'What is sex?'

'What is sex?'

Why, I asked myself, do adults always repeat questions when they don't know what to say?

I repeated, 'What *is* sex?'

Freddy looked totally floored. 'How do you mean?'

'What is it?'

He thought hard and came up with, 'Sex is life.'

'Does that mean that people who don't have sex are dead?'

'I guess so, yes.'

'How come, then, that children have a lot more life than adults, and children don't have sex?'

'Sex is happiness and pleasure then.'

'How come that children are a lot happier and have a lot more pleasure than adults and they don't have sex?'

'Children are easily pleased I guess.'

D1549675

DELICATE MATTERS

Vickery Turner

WARNER BOOKS

A *Warner* Book

First published in Great Britain
in 1995 by Little, Brown and Company
This edition published in 1996 by Warner Books

Copyright © Vickery Turner 1995

The moral right of the author has been asserted.

*All characters in this publication are fictitious
and any resemblance to real persons, living or dead,
is purely coincidental.*

All rights reserved.
No part of this publication may be reproduced,
stored in a retrieval system, or transmitted, in any
form or by any means, without the prior
permission in writing of the publisher, nor be
otherwise circulated in any form of binding or
cover other than that in which it is published and
without a similar condition including this
condition being imposed on the subsequent purchaser.

A CIP catalogue record for this book
is available from the British Library.

ISBN 0 7515 1162 5

Printed and bound in Great Britain by Clays Ltd, St Ives plc

Warner Books
A Division of
Little, Brown and Company (UK)
Brettenham House
Lancaster Place
London WC2E 7EN

DELICATE MATTERS

CHAPTER

1

It's been a crowded two years. They say that when the years start flashing by you're getting old. I started to get old the April before last, when I was thirteen. After that there was no more watching the clouds float by in endless summers and eternal days.

I spent most of that year mourning the loss of my bedroom. Freddy had arrived in a U-Haul van full of photographic equipment and taken over my room because my mother could not afford the rent. He moved my plastic mermaids and ducks out of the bath and filled it with sodium hyposulphate for developing films, so we had to negotiate with him when we wanted to have a bath.

During my thirteenth year they boarded up the bridge leading from our little ghetto in the western puddles of London to the sanctified pavements of Holland Park. It remained boarded up for months while hidden men did mysterious things with pneumatic drills and high-pressure hoses. Cars had to make wide detours around Olympia or Shepherd's Bush. Pedestrians had to walk in single file along the meagre alley provided, where they were nudged by impatient cyclists balancing on wobbling bicycles.

Our flat was in a no-go area according to Grandma Eunice, because there were dustbins on every doorstep

1

along our street, a blight which, for her, was a portent of muggers, rapists and drug traffickers. After her initial visit she refused to come any more, but made up for it with phone calls, which really annoyed Freddy.

'Tell that woman to cool it,' he said. 'Every time the phone rings, my heart skips a beat because I think it's my agent.'

To which I replied, 'I don't believe you have a heart or an agent.'

And he said, 'Shut your mouth, Fatso.' Which was the kind of thing he used to say to provide me with an aggressive masculine influence.

'Nobody with a heart would make a remark like that to someone who's struggling with a few pounds.'

Freddy and I were always arguing. It was a power struggle of sorts. I was used to having my own way with everything and he didn't think I should. It was his habit to act tough with me because he thought my mother was too weak and let me push her around too much. It was not my fault that she was weak but it meant that I had to put up with Freddy acting like a sergeant major. He would shout at me if I left a dirty plate in the sink without rinsing it first, something I'd been doing for years. And he would tell me to empty the kitchen bin but I always wore him down in a waiting game. My trick was never to see or smell rotting garbage. I was immune to it. Freddy was not.

He was the first one I interviewed. It was not an easy task. To obtain the interview I had to battle my way into his room across a moat of trunks, electric cables, tripods, umbrella lights and skiing equipment which he had put there to prevent my mother and me from asking his advice. And then I had to duck under a black plastic sheet hanging over his door to keep us and the light out.

Freddy was not pleased to see me standing there with my

clipboard and tape recorder. He sighed and said, 'What do you want?'

He bore a striking resemblance to the Russian army officer Pyotr Aleksandrovich Rumyanysev, Count Zadunaysky, as pictured in volume ten of my Encyclopaedia Britannica, that is, if you took away the white wig and double chin. Freddy had thick, dark curly hair that sat on his head like a ripe blackberry, and he was, I believe, thirty-one when he came to live with us.

I put my tape recorder on his bed, pressed 'record', and said, 'I'm here to interview you for Sex 2000, my social studies project. It's a survey. I believe your name is Frederick Lunn Tatham, is that correct?'

Freddy pressed the stop button. 'You're doing what?'

'Freddy! You promised. I don't know who else to interview.' I was whining.

'For God's sake, Jane, you can't do a survey if you're only going to interview one person.'

'I'm going to ask Grandma Eunice and I'm going to look for opportunities. Anyway it's not really a survey, it's a consumer report.'

'On sex?'

'Yes.'

'You can't do a consumer report on sex.'

'That's what our teacher said, but we talked her round.'

'Why don't you choose another subject? Sex has been done to death.'

'No. I don't want to. It's topical. I was the first one in my class who had the guts to say I'd do it.'

'I wouldn't call it guts, Jane.'

'Maybe you wouldn't.'

He was sitting on his navy-blue Ralph Lauren sheets looking at photo proofs and eating a chicken sandwich. He alternated between being an actor and a photographer. That particular week he had landed a bonanza photographic job which explained why he had gone up to Bond Street and bought the expensive sheets.

I pressed the recording button again. 'I believe your name is Frederick Lunn Tatham?'

He pressed the stop button. 'Cut it out. Do you think I'm going to let you play a recording at school about my sex life with my name all over it?'

'OK. No names. I won't say who you are.'

He wanted to get back to his photo proofs. If he started saying he had a deadline I was going to ask him why he sat on the sofa half the morning watching *Thunderbirds* and *The Invaders*.

'I promise you, Freddy. I'm not going to play the tape at school. It's for reference only. I'm going to write it all out.'

After all that, the interview was quite short. He didn't look up once because he was going through his proofs of a red-haired girl in a fuchsia chiffon dress. Her eyes were closed in a lot of them. The subjects in Freddy's photographs often looked unprepared because he snapped the shutter too fast, like a mad soldier with an automatic rifle, bam, bam, bam. He thought it made for realism but most of the time it made for crooked mouths, eyes closed or squinting, and hair over the face.

The interview went like this.

'Am I right in believing that you are not a heterosexual?'

'Yes, Jane, you are correct in that.'

'You are, as they say, homosexual?'

'You've hit it right on the nosey.'

'Are you pleased about that?'

'I'm neither pleased nor unpleased. It's a fact of life.'

'What advice do you have to give me about sex?'

'Advice?'

4

'Yes. I'm thirteen years old and I need to know something about it.'

'You want my advice?'

'Yes.'

'I'd say be honest.'

'How can I be honest about something I don't know anything about?'

'You will.'

'Sophia had her fourteenth birthday last week and she gets drunk at parties and she gets really close to doing "it". What do you think about that?'

'Well I'm not a great one for holding back the tide, if you know what I mean.'

'What is sex?'

'What is sex?'

Why, I asked myself, do adults always repeat questions when they don't know what to say?

I repeated, 'What is sex?'

Freddy looked totally floored. 'How do you mean?'

'What *is* it?'

He thought hard and then came up with, 'Sex is life.'

'Does that mean that people who don't have sex are dead?'

'I guess so, yes.'

'How come, then, that children have a lot more life than adults, and children don't have sex?'

'Sex is happiness and pleasure then.'

'How come that children are a lot happier and have a lot more pleasure than adults and they don't have sex?'

'Children are easily pleased I guess.'

After that Freddy had a phone call from his agent about an audition for a low-budget movie and I had to climb back over the cables, tripods and umbrella lights. Actors get very intense when they talk to their agents and they don't like to be distracted.

I went back to my bedroom, or rather, my shelf. I was always complaining to Freddy, 'Since you came here I've had to live on a shelf. No one should have to live on a shelf, not even a dog.'

When I said a shelf, I meant that there were virtually no floor spaces left in the bedroom I shared with my mother. When Freddy moved in, all my furniture was moved into my mother's already overcrowded room. Furniture was wedged together until it formed an almost unbroken surface with three deep potholes leading to the carpet miles below. To get from the door to the window I had to leap like a mountain goat over two chests of drawers, across the bed, over a white wicker nightstand and across my desk which was wedged with drawers inaccessible against the window frame. Lying in bed at night was like being the central part of a difficult jigsaw puzzle.

I used to lie there and plot my next move with my Sex 2000 project. Let me say here in my own defence that I conducted that consumer report two years ago and I am a lot older now. I have absolutely no relationship to that adolescent girl who went around embarrassing people and asking all those immature questions and causing all the trouble that I caused.

I had no idea that sex was such a touchy subject. I was more naïve than most thirteen-year-olds, I suppose. Well, I know I was. I disown her. She has nothing to do with me.

CHAPTER

2

I was not going to waste my time or pocket money on the charity ball but Sophia said it was an important mating ritual to observe and would be useful for my Sex 2000 project.

'What shall I wear?' I asked her.

'Anything from Miss Selfridge or Top Shop that's really tight or really short. Or otherwise you can go to Harrods or Harvey Nichols for a flouncy, strapless number but the trouble with that kind of dress is you're stuck with it, you can't wear it round the pubs in Chiswick on a Saturday night.'

Sophia's father was a South African executive of something or other and her mother was a brittle, chain-smoking Frenchwoman with a beautiful face and a wrinkled mouth. They lived in an ancient waterfront cottage in Chiswick, very English and rose covered, with every electric labour-saving device and fancy gadget you could imagine. Sophia's bedroom was covered in posters of Keanu Reeves and Ethan Hawke, which my bedroom would have been covered with too, if I'd had a bedroom.

Sophia and I had been thrown together because we were currently out of fashion at school. Nobody gained prestige points from hanging around with us, which made us social pariahs. Why we were unfashionable was a complete mystery to me; if I'd known why, I would have done something about it. Sophia and I spent hours discussing why we were unacceptable but we never came to any brilliant conclusions.

Personally I couldn't stand her, but she was all I had and she knew a lot about the faster side of life. She frequently trolled up and down the pubs along the riverfront and bought shandies and smoked cigarettes and got mistaken for being eighteen. She was already fourteen, eight months older than me, but she'd packed a lot into those eight months and I knew I would have to work very hard to catch up with her – if I wanted to.

'Come round to my house and my dad will drive us over, OK?'

I arrived at her cottage wearing a black dress I had bought from Top Shop for twenty pounds the year before. I had thought at the time that it was terrifyingly sophisticated but Sophia said it was out of date and made me try on one of her skimpy hot pink Kookai dresses.

I was larger than she was and could not get it over my shoulders.

'Step into it,' she ordered. 'Pull it up.'

I tried. 'Ugh! It's pushing my hips up to my nose.'

'Persevere. You have to suffer to look beautiful.'

'I don't have to look beautiful. I'm going for research purposes.'

'You have to live. Come on. Push harder.'

'Ugh!' I pulled the dress into place, somehow got my arms into the sleeves and surveyed myself in the mirror.

'You look fantastic,' said Sophia.

'I can't breathe.'

'That's good. It'll make you sound breathy, like Marilyn Monroe.'

The dress was so tight that it was like a hot pink corset. It held everything in.

'It's crushing my ribs, Sophia. I'll die.'

'No you won't. You need hot pink lipstick and earrings.'

'I don't have any holes in my ears.'

'I'll do it for you now. All you need is some ice and a needle. You won't feel a thing.'

'My mother doesn't want me mutilated until I'm at least sixteen.'

'She won't notice. Wear your hair over your ears.'

'My mother notices everything. She knows everything I've done the minute I walk in the room.'

Sophia looked extremely sympathetic. 'My God, how bloody awful for you. If my parents could do that I'd have been hung, drawn and quartered years ago.'

Sophia's father, a genial, remote man, drove us to Bayswater in a car with nice cream leather upholstery. He said, 'Have a nice party, girls,' and purred away, leaving us in the rain with a lot of public-school boys in evening dress.

'Come on,' said Sophia and pulled me up the steps.

I remember the rest of the evening as being extremely painful. I had not had a great deal of contact with the opposite sex and had resorted to watching *Stand By Me*, the classic film about twelve-year-old boys, to understand what the opposite sex thought and talked about. I had watched it over and over and knew every line by heart but it offered no help now I was confronted with live, breathing youths tearing off their jackets and ties.

A boy came up to Sophia and said, 'Do you like Rage Against the Machine?'

And she said, 'Yes.'

So he said, 'Do you want to go upstairs?'

She said, 'Yes.'

So they went up to the balcony and got off, that is, they

did some violent snogging and then they came down the stairs again. She never did find out his name.

'How was it?' I asked her.

'Well the trouble with boys from Eton is that they haven't a clue,' she said.

'How do you know he was from Eton?' I asked.

'Because he hadn't a clue. They're locked up in that school all term and then they try to fit a term into one evening. They think girls are Easter eggs. They need some boys from Holland Park Comprehensive here to show them how to relate.'

Nobody asked me to dance even though my hot pink dress had steadily shrunk concertina style towards my armpits, but I expect the fact that I glared at my feet the entire evening did not help.

It was not fashionable to say you hadn't had a fabulous time at the ball because it would have indicated that you were a social failure, immature and not ready for the high life. So everybody swore that they had had the most hilarious time and it was not until a year or two later that anyone admitted they had hated it.

CHAPTER

3

My mother spent half the morning trying to figure out what to wear to the funeral: black velvet jacket with black velvet skirt – too velvety, too black and marred by spots of green paint on the cuffs; brown linen jacket – too crumpled; brown tweed jacket – too horsy. The bed was littered with clothes when she came up with an old brown Laura Ashley dress under a stretched out black cardigan with large pockets.

She had been, in her usual nervous, compulsive way, in the habit of pushing her hands deep into the cardigan pockets and wrapping them tightly around her chest, so that it now had an elongated front which almost reached her knees, whereas at the back it came only to her waist.

I had never been to a funeral before so I had no idea what to expect. I knew that at state funerals presidents often got together to negotiate, so I took along my tape recorder in case the opportunity arose to interview my grandmother about her sex life. That was the first of the many really stupid things I did.

I repeat my disclaimer. I take no responsibility for the actions of this ridiculously immature girl.

When I sat next to Grandma Eunice I could feel the sleeve of her silk suit tickling like a ladybird crawling up my arm. I loved anything silky, velvety, satiny. For many years my best friend was a yellow baby-blanket from Boots the Chemists. I loved its hypnotically soft, shiny border and its comforting wool.

I lost it on a camping trip in Cornwall when I was eight. My father (more of him later) said I was too old to get another blanket. My mother said she could not afford to get one because, by then, my father had left her and she had no money for anything.

So I had to cope with a lacy jumper that my mother never finished knitting, together with a nylon waist petticoat I had worn when I was four. It was hard trying to recreate the exact sensation of that perfect, soft, wonderful Boots blanket, but by holding the two articles in a tight grip I could pretend they were one and be swept away to my blanket days. They were still in active use when I was thirteen.

We were late to Grandpa Cyrus' funeral because there was a lot of traffic around Clapham Common and my mother was in the wrong lane. This was more of a problem than it was with most drivers because once my mother settled in a lane she rarely had the courage to change out of it. If I hadn't shouted at her we would have gone on circling Clapham Common forever.

By the time we arrived at the service they were on the last verse of 'Onward Christian Soldiers'. We were attempting to creep into the back row when Grandma Eunice, who was on the lookout in the front pew, turned and beckoned us vigorously. The music stopped, they all sat down, silence reigned and Eunice continued to beckon. Everyone turned to have a good look at the two latecomers. We had to walk up to the front in an awesome silence, watched by a multitude of red, wet eyes. It was excruciatingly painful for me and absolute death for my mother.

The vicar, who had been planning to speak, decided instead to join the others in watching us proceed up the aisle. There was a small space at the end of the front pew next to a large sobbing woman in a loose, tent-like orange garment. We swooped down on it, glad to be out of the limelight. I sat with my tape recorder on my knee and had a few seconds to study the pattern of green ballerinas doing pirouettes, glissades and pliés on the orange tent before Eunice leaned over and said, 'Change places with her. I don't want anyone to think she's my daughter.'

My mother whispered as quietly as she could behind the sobbing woman's head, 'Isn't she one of Cyrus' relatives?'

'How should I know? He had a lot of relatives,' said Eunice.

'What shall I say?'

Eunice looked exasperated. 'Tell her you want to sit next to your mother.'

The vicar was reading from the book of Revelation as the plump lady's hoop earrings rattled in time with her sobs and we squeezed past her large knees. At one point I sat on her lap and dropped my tape recorder on the floor.

When we finally landed next to Eunice and my mother's sister, Joanna, it was immediately obvious that our troubles were not over. Eunice was wearing an ultra chic, black silk designer suit and a midnight black hat with a veil over her expensively coiffured baby blonde hair. And Joanna, like an apprentice vulture, was wearing an identical black suit and hat.

They both stared at my mother's baggy cardigan.

'Where did you drag that up from?' asked Eunice. 'Oxfam?'

'Don't you have anything classic?' whispered Joanna.

To which my mother replied, 'I thought it was suitable for the occasion.'

They twittered with annoyance. Luckily, my mother was saved by the arrival of another latecomer, a tall, silver-haired man who hovered by the door for a few seconds and then ducked into a back pew.

'That's Frank Sherman,' said Eunice. 'He was in the Navy with Cyrus.'

Joanna craned her neck to see.

'He's a widower,' added Eunice. 'She left him half of Queensland in her will.'

'No kidding!' said Joanna, straining harder to catch a glimpse.

'Half of Queensland!' I whispered in amazement to my mother.

'She doesn't mean half,' said my mother.

The congregation rose to sing 'Abide with Me' which made everyone cry. In the midst of their grief Eunice and Joanna continued to peer over their shoulders at the wealthy Frank Sherman in the back row, while my mother fiddled with her cardigan and tried to pull it into shape.

When it was all over everyone went outside and looked at the bouquets and wreaths in the drizzling rain. Eunice and Joanna sought shelter under a tree, where they received condolences from fellow mourners. Eunice's eyes filled with tears which shimmied down her cheeks, making little rivulets of shiny skin through her powdery make-up.

'I hardly got to know him,' she said. 'He was my last ditch stand.'

At the time I was not quite sure what last ditch stand meant but I knew that Grandpa Cyrus was her fifth husband so I assumed it meant that she had reached her quota.

The rain filtered down through the leaves of the huge sycamore over our heads and joined the tears on Eunice's face. So to cheer her up I said, 'I'm doing a project for my social studies class.'

She patted her face carefully with a lace handkerchief. 'Are you dear? What about?'

'Well Mrs Cassels said we should look at the last decade of the century and do a consumer report on an item of our choice like Food 2000, Transport 2000, or Fashion 2000. I'm doing Sex 2000.'

Eunice's lace handkerchief became motionless for a few seconds while she threw a sharp look at my mother. The sharp look plunged like a knife into my mother's navel: she looked wounded, pushed her hands deep into her woollen cardigan pockets and wrapped them protectively around her stomach, stretching the cardigan further out of shape.

'Sex 2000?' asked Eunice. 'Did you know about this?'

'Yes,' my mother answered doubtfully, as if she didn't know.

My grandmother scrutinised me carefully like someone about to purchase a flea-ridden puppy. 'How old are you now?'

'I'll be fourteen in November.'

'So you're thirteen.'

'Yes,' I said. 'I'd like to interview you as an older, experienced woman. I could ask you a couple of questions now if you like. I've got my tape recorder. It's an important topic. I could ask you what you think sex has to offer young people today and how it will change as we start a new century. Just a couple of questions. It will cheer you up.'

Eunice stared at me, stone-faced. 'I don't want to be cheered up.'

'Let Grandma be miserable,' my mother whispered.

So after that we hung around under the trees in silence. The cold, moist air mottled blue patches on my hands and legs and made the other mourners clutch at their clothes. A freezing wind blew over the ancient gravestones and rattled the petals off the florists' arrangements lying in the wet grass. My mother shivered nervously in her Laura Ashley dress and misshapen cardigan. She shifted impatiently from one foot to the other which, I knew, meant she was worrying about being late to work.

'I have to go to work now,' she whispered apologetically to my grandmother as everyone prepared to leave the cemetery and go to Joanna's mothbally flat in Dolphin Square.

These words gave Eunice another reason to grieve and she stared abjectly at my mother. 'You're not still working at that place are you? You can't go at a time like this. We all have to rally round. Joanna's prepared lunch. Smoked salmon, prawn vol-au-vents, chocolate layer cake.'

'I can't come,' said my mother miserably.

'It sounds wonderful,' I said, trying to be positive. 'I love Joanna's chocolate layer cake. Maybe we could come after work.'

But Eunice went on staring at my mother, 'I never thought I'd live to see my own daughter working as a washerwoman,' she said.

My mother twisted her foot round her ankle. 'I just do a few service washes, that's all.'

'Service washes!' Eunice spat the words out in disgust.

A cold blast of wind came rushing through the mossy gravestones and seemed to bite our skin with sharp teeth. My mother was shivering and examining her hands with great interest and obviously did not have a clue what to say. As she was hopeless at defending herself I had developed the habit of helping my mother in times of need. So I said brightly, 'Do you believe in life after death Grandma?'

'Yes.'

'Then it sounds as if you're going to give Grandpa Cyrus a great going away party.'

Eunice's eyes filled with tears all over again and she wept in a most distressed manner. I knew she would. But it meant that we could make our escape. My mother felt guilty about it. She felt guilty about everything.

SEX 2000 – CONSUMER REPORT

Subject – Virginity.

Object – To study virginity for its comfort, convenience, durability, satisfaction, performance, benefit, design, workmanship, value and strength.

It was all Sophia's fault. Mrs Cassels had been telling our class how to conduct a thorough consumer report on an item such as a shirt which would be included in the consumer survey Fashion 2000. And out of the blue Sophia said that if we were going to do a comprehensive look at the last decade of the twentieth century, we should not just look at fashion, travel and food but we should also look into sex. Mrs Cassels explained that sex could not be tested as a consumer item. And frankly I could see that she was right.

But Sophia and a couple of other girls had argued that sex was an important topic for us all to know more about. And then Sophia, bored as usual, dared me to say I would do it. And that was that. I went on record as the one who would take on Sex 2000. Mrs Cassels looked very unhappy but she did not want to look like an old prude, so she was stuck with it. And so was I.

Sophia told me during our lunch break. 'I don't really think you can do a consumer report on virginity.'

This really annoyed me. 'Sophia!' I wailed. 'You're the one who talked me into doing it in the first place.'

'All I'm saying,' said Sophia in that annoying, know-it-all way of hers, 'is that you can test a shirt for design and workmanship, but you can't test virginity.'

'That's exactly what Mrs Cassels said,' I wailed louder than ever. It was a tragedy that Sophia was my only friend. She was so unreliable.

'I think,' she said airily, 'that you should just ask people in possession of the item, virginity that is, what they are planning to do with it. Then you can weigh up their answers and get a few clues about its design and workmanship.'

'All right,' I asked, 'what are you planning to do with your virginity?'

Sophia gave it a couple of seconds thought and then said, 'As soon as I get into a stable relationship I'm going to dump my virginity because it's giving me a stale feeling.'

'*As soon* as you get into a stable relationship?'

'Yes.'

'How will you know it's stable if you've only just got into it?'

'I guess I'll wait until I know it's stable.'

'How long?'

'Two weeks?' suggested Sophia.

'Yes,' I said, 'Two weeks sounds good – I suppose.'

Conclusion: Under 'durability' I wrote, 'two weeks'.

CHAPTER
4

Once again my mother had difficulty getting out of her lane when circling Clapham Common and then found it impossible to get off the A3. We ended up following a red Volkswagen on an unnecessary detour over Wimbledon Common and listening to an American psychologist, Dr Arnold Jefferies, on the radio who was pushing his book, *The Killer Instinct and You*.

My mother listened very intently when the psychologist insisted that anyone could learn the killer instinct, that it was not an instinct at all, but a set of scientific rules to be followed.

'Tape it! Tape it!' my mother said, waving her hand at the radio as we drifted towards Kingston like a tram stuck in the wrong lines.

There was no cassette recorder attached to the radio in our Hillman Imp but my mother kept on waving her hand at the radio, expecting some kind of magic to happen. So I held my own little battery operated recorder close to the radio and made a really bad recording, hardly audible with a lot of whirring engine noise in the background.

We were even later than planned getting to Vincent's Coachworks. Vincent owned the far end of an alley off the Goldhawk Road. He did panel beating, chassis repairs, welding and respraying on any car that could make it through the heaps of old rubble lined up along the alley. Tyres, steering wheels, hoses, rusty exhaust pipes, bucket seats, twisted bumpers, dashboards and doors were kept by Vincent for his other occupation – restoring cars that had been destroyed and written off after a crash and selling them to unsuspecting customers. The vast array of strewn car parts presented an almost impenetrable obstacle course to any newcomer. Once a customer had figured out the wild zig-zag course required to get to the end of the alley it was not too difficult to repeat it, but it needed experience.

The last door in the alley led, via a passage, to the back end of Vincent's launderette. Customers taking their washing to the launderette entered it from a door in an adjacent street and knew nothing of the constant welding and spraying in the body shop beyond.

As we drove up the alley my mother was patting her short bobbed hair into place as though preparing to meet royalty. And she was apologising before she had opened the car door.

'I'm sorry, it was my stepfather's funeral.' She sounded out of breath as she stepped out on to the narrow strip of oil-stained cobblestones that lay in front of the reception office.

Vincent was examining the dented rear end and smashed tail light of a brand new Ford Escort XRI. Apart from the damaged area the car was an immaculate spotless black, with a brilliant almost mirror-like sheen and a thin gold stripe running from front to back. The owner, an unEnglish-looking man in pale corduroy trousers and rimless glasses, leaned resignedly against the office door. I thought at first he was French or Scandinavian because he seemed slightly different.

'It's twelve-fifteen.' Vincent scowled. 'Funerals don't take all day. The phone's been ringing. I've been running up and down this bloody alley the whole bloody morning.' He straightened his back and winced accusingly as though it were my mother's fault. He was wearing the blue overalls that used to fit before he gained the extra thirty pounds that were now squeezed like sausage meat into a sock. His wispy red hair was scraped back from his almost bald head and tied with a tight rubber band into a skimpy pony tail, which looked like a piece of string on a balloon.

He began shouting at my mother, 'This is a business we're running here! Don't tell me you can't make it on time.' Vincent's eyes flicked over to the customer to see if he was watching. He loved an audience.

My mother blushed. She was always blushing. She would even blush on someone else's behalf because she totally identified with embarrassed people.

'Well . . . I'll get on with it,' she said. The customer leaning on the office door moved out of the way as she headed towards it.

'We've got a recession on here,' Vincent shouted. 'There's people starving on the streets and if you can't make it on time then get your arse out of here and I'll get someone else.'

My mother twitched her mouth into smile position as though she thought Vincent was being a little theatrical. Her hand froze on the office door knob and I could tell she didn't know what to do or say.

So I said, 'Oh, Vincent . . .'

'What?'

I was thinking about saying there had been a terrible accident on Hammersmith Bridge and we were stuck there for an hour, but before the words came out, I noticed my tape recorder on the front seat of the Hillman Imp. So instead I found myself saying, 'Could I interview you for a school project?'

'Not now. Can't you see I've got a customer?'

'Yes, but afterwards . . .'

'What's it about?'

'It's a survey called Sex 2000. That means sex now and how it will develop in the next century.'

'Sex? Is that what you're studying at that fancy school?'

My mother slipped quietly into the office and closed the door behind her. Vincent paid no attention. He was thoroughly distracted.

'It's a survey,' I repeated. 'I chose the topic. I chose Travel 2000 first but then I changed my mind.'

'So you want to hear it from a male chauvinist pig?' Vincent grinned at the customer who stared back at him clinically through his rimless glasses. 'Get it from the expert.'

He turned back to the customer. 'When I was at school we studied reading, writing and arithmetic, now they study sex. No wonder the country's in such poor shape.' He leaned over to pick glass out of the broken tail light which was hanging like a half-extracted tooth. 'But come to think of it, if a few of my girlfriends had studied sex at school I wouldn't have had to work so hard getting them to come across.' Vincent snickered.

The customer was not all that interested in what Vincent had to say about his sex life. 'How much will it cost and how long will it take?' The man had an American accent.

Vincent wiped some grease off his nose and pointed at the car's fancy gold racing stripe. 'The stripe's the problem. The stripe could take a week, two weeks. Have to send away for it. I can get the rest done by Thursday. If you leave it till Saturday we might have the stripe.' He took a breath. 'Eight hundred and fifty, plus VAT.'

'Aaagh,' said the customer, swallowing poisonous medicine. 'I was just waiting at a stop-light minding my own business. And this guy comes along ... he said he was insured, but I don't know if I believe him.'

'Well there you go.' Vincent was unsympathetic; he hated it when people cried on his shoulder. 'Louise!' he yelled, like he was shouting 'Timber!' 'Get this customer's details.'

He picked up his wrench and went up the alley, stepping expertly through the littered bones of extinct cars. I did not want a potential interviewee to escape so I ran after him. 'Vincent!'

But he would not stop. He continued on his way singing in a tuneless, croaky voice, 'Let's talk about sex, baby,' and swivelling his hips in time to the beat.

I was going to continue my pursuit but I noticed a boy about my age waiting to talk to him outside the body shop. There had been one or two boys around of late because Vincent had put an ad in the local newsagents for a Saturday worker. I caught a flash of a gold earring and concluded that the boy was one of those street-wise types who would really despise me if I didn't act the right way. So I went across the alley to the office.

The reception office was a fancy title for an old stable-cum-garage where Vincent kept his files and paperwork, plus, to the discerning eye, a better class of rubble than the selection in the alley. Here were kept his more choice pieces under the protection of a roof.

There was a pathway through these less torn bucket seats and less rusty exhaust pipes to a counter where the American customer was filling out a form, muttering to himself as he attempted to come up with the right answers. When he had completed it he pushed the form distastefully across the counter.

23

'What a disaster,' he glowered. 'It all happens at once. My kitchen flooded this morning, washing machine went berserk.'

'We have a launderette here,' I said helpfully. 'We do service washes.'

He did not appear grateful for the information. 'Do you collect it?' he asked suspiciously.

'No, but sometimes we deliver it afterwards.'

'Then why don't you collect it?' The concept really irritated him.

'I don't know.'

My mother, who by then had gathered her wits and was looking reasonably pale and composed, took the form. She had only looked at it for about two seconds when a pink tide washed right over her face, coming up from her neck, until her whole face was a bright raspberry colour.

I leaned over the counter to see what on earth he had written that was so terrible and discovered that the offending words were at the top of the form. Under 'name' he had put ARNOLD DAVID JEFFERIES.

We had a celebrity in our office! We should have recognised his voice. It was the Dr Arnold Jefferies we had heard on LBC radio as we were drifting along the A3 less than an hour before!

How did he find out about Vincent's Coachworks? It was not a place that celebrities knew about. When did he have the accident? Was it before or after the radio programme?

At this point most mothers would have asked, 'Are you the Dr Arnold Jefferies I heard on the radio this morning? Did you write *The Killer Instinct and You?*'

But my mother was not most mothers. She kept her head down and focused on some papers on the counter that she shuffled intently. All she said was, 'Thank you, Dr Jefferies,' which was a dead giveaway because he had not written Dr on the form. So he knew that she knew, but he did not say anything either.

It was all in the subtext. I did not fully understand then but I know now that most of adult life takes place in the subtext. As for example in *The Three Sisters* when Tusenbach tells Irina, 'I didn't have any coffee this morning,' when what he really means is, 'I want to look at you one more time because I'm going to go off now and allow myself to get shot in a duel.'

Adults live in their subtext which is a polite way of saying they lie all the time.

Dr Arnold Jefferies had thick brown hair growing in clumps that sprouted uncertainly in different directions. His faded corduroys and rimless glasses were not alone in giving him an academic appearance. It was easy to tell from the slightly bad-tempered, aloof way he filled out his form that he considered that he had higher intellectual pursuits to follow than form filling. I knew he was the man on the radio programme because his voice was identical. He had been rather cocky with the interviewer and acted as though he were doing him a great favour by appearing on his show. But he was not all that great looking. He certainly wasn't as immaculate as his car, even with the big dent in it.

My mother and I went outside to watch him drive off in a green Honda Civic that he had borrowed from the office. It was the one with the cigarette burn in the back seat that I had pried open with my little finger into a considerable hole.

'Phew!' said my mother as if she'd had a narrow escape. Then she saw Vincent coming towards the office and she ducked back inside and began shuffling papers quickly.

SEX 2000 – CONSUMER REPORT

Sex – its value in communication.

Conducting my consumer report among my peers was ridden with obstacles. There were various girls in my class who knew a lot more about sex than I did, but they would not talk to me because of my lack of status. They would not reply to my inquiries about how much of an asset sex was in communication. There were no points to be gained from being seen with me. So I asked Sophia during our maths lesson how valuable she thought sex was as a way of getting to know people.

Sophia informed me, 'You have to have sex if you really want to know somebody. Up to the point of sex everyone's a mystery. Then Whammy! You have sex and the person's an open book. You've uncovered their psychic mystery.'

'Don't you think,' I asked, 'that a really long conversation would cover the same ground?'

I received a withering look from Sophia.

'But really,' I insisted, 'there must be other ways. What if you got stuck in a lift with somebody? Or you went on a Duke of Edinburgh course to the Peak District? You know, saw them under stress?'

'Stress can't compete with sex.'

'I think it can.'

'Well you're wrong.'

'Tell me this then. If you have a lot of sex with someone do you get to know them better than anyone else?'

'Of course, the more sex, the more you know them,' said Sophia.

'That might not be a good idea. You might find out too much.'

Mrs Wilbur, the maths teacher, stared beadily and said, 'Jane, what did I just say?'

I had to wait until my next lesson before I wrote my conclusion.

Conclusion: Sex is an extremely useful way to get to know people if you don't have time to go on a Duke of Edinburgh course in the Peak District. If you have too much time for sex, as in the case of many parents, you get to know your partner too well and divorce sets in.

CHAPTER

5

Five minutes after it had rattled away from Vincent's Coachworks the green Honda Civic, with Dr Jefferies still at the wheel, reappeared at the end of the alley and rattled towards us at a very fast rate, swaying and scraping its way through Vincent's piles of car bones. The car bounced against a chicane of tyres and then seemed to ricochet from one side of the alley to another, almost hitting the walls.

Vincent watched in annoyance. 'That bloke scratches my Honda then he'll have to pay for it.'

The Honda skidded to a halt. Dr Jefferies jumped out and ran at a frantic pace to his Escort, where he rattled and tugged at the handle of the boot.

'It won't open till I fix it,' yelled Vincent loudly. Then quietly he said, 'Stupid git.'

Vincent spat an imaginary speck of something on to the gravel and walked slowly to the Honda, where he ran his hand searchingly over its smooth surface. Satisfied that the Honda's greenness was intact, he strolled over to the anxious customer. 'What's the trouble?'

Without looking up from his incessant tugging, Dr Jefferies said, 'I left something in the trunk.'

'Well, it'll have to stay there for a couple of days. I can't get round to it today.'

Dr Jefferies looked up and gave Vincent what I supposed was a killer instinct look, then he gave the boot handle an almighty pull and it opened about three inches.

'Don't force it,' said Vincent sharply. 'You'll break the . . .'

Dr Jefferies strained and pushed until the boot was wide open. Vincent was now totally cheesed off but he watched with curiosity as the customer leaned into the boot and pulled out a large cage.

'I don't know where my head was at. Sorry, guys,' Dr Jefferies said to the cage. He held it close to his chest, cradling it like a baby, and studying the interior with deep concern. Then he lowered it slowly on to the ground and crouched down to look inside.

After a few moments he said, 'Whaddyaknow. No sign of stress. No reaction whatsoever. That's education.' He sat back on his heels and looked up with a relieved half-smile on his face. He did not look like the sort of person who smiled all that often.

Vincent closed in to get a better view of the interior of the cage and I followed. We saw about a dozen rats; velvety white rats with pink noses were in preponderance but there were two or three greyish brown among them. They looked relaxed, as far as I could make out. I had no idea what a stressed out rat looked like. Dr Jefferies got off his haunches and lifted the cage into the Honda Civic.

'If you want rats,' said Vincent, 'I've got some up the alley behind the shed. Genuine Shepherd's Bush rats. Pedigree.'

'No thanks,' said Dr Jefferies coolly and rattled away before Vincent could change his mind about the loan of the Honda.

CHAPTER

6

When I pressed the monitor button on the phone in the kitchen Grandma Eunice was saying to my mother, 'You must understand, Louise, I'm a widow. The eyes of the world are upon me.'

I kept the monitor button switched on and listened. I was not being nosey, I was waiting to interview Eunice. I thought that now she'd had a week to recover from the funeral she would be more receptive to a Sex 2000 interview. If, as Freddy said, sex was life, then it would help remove the spectre of death.

'But I can't move out of this flat,' said my mother. 'I have nowhere to go.'

So Eunice had ordered my mother to leave the flat. I had seen that coming for a long time. She was firmly convinced that we should escape the dustbins of Hammersmith and live in Holland Park like her.

'Get some money out of Richard,' commanded Eunice.

Everyone said that. No one could understand why my mother had to struggle when my father appeared to be so comfortable.

'I've told you, Richard's broke.'

'Broke! Pull the other one. He's living in Chelsea Harbour.'

'Near Chelsea Harbour.'

'Near it. In it. He doesn't live in a dangerous ghetto.'

'It's not dangerous. And we've made it very comfortable here,' said my mother doubtfully.

'How can you be comfortable? You have a lodger. You've turned Jane out of her room. She shouldn't be sleeping with her mother. She's not a refugee.'

'I know. In an ideal world she wouldn't be but you can't criticise Richard. He's paying the school fees, they cost a fortune.'

'You don't like asking him for money. It's a natural thing to ask a man for money. They appreciate it, and it makes them feel big. You'll have to snap out of it, Louise, there's a lot more at stake here than meets the eye.'

'What do you mean by that?'

'I mean what I say. I'm trying to forge a future for myself.'

At that moment Freddy, in dark blue Bermuda shorts and white T-shirt, returned to the kitchen after taking the rubbish out to the dustbin. He recognised the voice on the monitor.

'Forge a future? Is she studying to be a blacksmith? Move over, Fatso.'

He cleared a space for himself and took two hard-boiled eggs out of his Le Creuset saucepan.

'What are you making, Freddy?'

'I'm making a sandwich for myself. This is not a canteen. I'm not feeding the public. If you want to eat, get off that chair and make yourself something.'

'It doesn't taste as good when I make it.'

'That's not my problem.'

'I'm having a dinner on Friday week,' Eunice said on the phone monitor. 'Richard's coming. I want you and Jane to come too.'

31

'Do I have to?' moaned my mother.

Freddy glanced at the red monitor button. 'Is it ethical to eavesdrop like this?'

'I'm not eavesdropping,' I replied. 'I'm waiting for a gap.'

'I don't want to sit there all night listening to Richard,' said my mother, sounding more distressed. 'He despises me. He makes me feel bad about myself.'

'But I need you to be there. Frank's coming.'

'Frank? Who's Frank?'

Eunice sighed. 'Who's Frank? You saw him on Saturday. How could you forget?'

'Frank,' I told Freddy, 'was at the funeral. He owns half of Queensland.'

'Send him over,' said Freddy, as he removed a tomato from a pan of hot water and peeled off the skin.

Eunice went from sighing to whining, a technique I recognised because I often tried it myself. 'Frank wants to meet you,' she whined. 'He wants to meet Jane, he wants to meet Richard. He wants to meet my family. He's interested in my family. You'll like him.'

'But . . .' My mother began to sound trepidatious, like someone talking to a lunatic holding a hatchet, 'Richard isn't your family anymore.'

'Frank doesn't know that,' said Eunice sharply.

'Why doesn't he know?'

'Because I didn't tell him and don't you go telling him either.'

'You can't make me do this.' My mother tried a puny, undersized whine. 'This is madness.'

'Call it what you like. I've made up my mind. I don't want Frank to think my daughter is divorced.'

'But why not? You're divorced.'

'Not anymore. I'm a widow. Frank knows I'm a widow.'

'What did I tell you?' said Freddy, slicing a ripe Haas

32

avocado. 'She's getting older so she's getting selective. Once she had five husbands. Now she can only remember the dead one. Next, she'll even forget that poor bastard and be a virgin.'

Eunice went on, 'I'm not handing him my entire résumé. No woman would ever get anywhere if she did that to a man. Frank's conservative, and conservative men put women on a pedestal, you know that, Louise.'

'Why do conservative men put women on a pedestal?' I asked Freddy.

'So they can vacuum the carpet? How should I know? I'm a Liberal Democrat.'

My mother was trying to raise her voice. 'I'm not coming.'

'Yes you are,' said Grandma Eunice. 'Have some sympathy. Look what I've been through, losing Cyrus so soon. How am I going to cope. It's a major coup getting Frank to come to dinner, he's always on a plane going somewhere. And don't tell him you're a washerwoman, say ... you do the occasional bit of charity work.'

'Why can't I tell him the truth?'

'Because it reeks of poverty. Rich people don't like being around poverty. They avoid it. And he's not going to avoid us.'

The phone call came to an unexpected end before I could speak up about my interview. My mother came into the kitchen with her hair pointing in strange peaks, the result of running her hands through it in frustration. She had been doing service washes all day and she was still wearing her pink overall with VINCENT'S LAUNDERETTE in red lettering on the pocket. She pulled a stool up to the counter, flopped on it wearily and watched Freddy rinsing endive and spring onions for his sandwich, a rapidly growing monument of vegetables, egg, cheeses and honey roast ham.

'Jane,' she asked weakly, putting tired, bony hands with transparent knuckles up to her face. 'Are you ashamed to tell your friends that you mother works in a launderette?'

'Discussing mothers is not big on the agenda,' I said. 'I could tell them anything. They don't listen. Freddy, can I have a bite of that?'

'No, you little turd. Make your own.'

I helped myself to two large bites, and went off to climb over the stepping stones of furniture in our bedroom to the phone, where I dialled my grandmother's number.

SEX 2000 – CONSUMER REPORT

Is sex user friendly?

Grandma Eunice was pleased to hear from me – at first.

When I explained that I had interviewed one man for my project and was hoping to trap a second, she was alarmed.

'Men? Grown-up men?'

'Yes. And now I feel I need a mature female approach for the sake of balance. Like I'd like to ask you as an experienced woman, have you found sex to be user friendly?'

'User friendly?' She spoke so sharply that her Yorkshire terrier, Bruce, began barking somewhere close to the phone. Eunice usually made her phone calls from the breakfast room overlooking her patio, where Bruce would sniff around the barrels of flowering shrubs. The flag-stoned patio led to a garden which provided a spring spectacle of daffodils, azaleas and forget-me-nots with not a weed in sight. Eunice had an exceptionally smart house and garden. She did not like half measures.

'Yes,' I replied. 'If you think of sex as a product like washing powder or toothpaste, would you recommend it to someone who hasn't tried it yet?'

There was a silence while Bruce barked, then she said, 'You're not going to talk like this in front of Frank are you?'

'Oh no. This is just between us. I'm like a priest or a doctor.'

'Well, Jane,' she sounded relieved, 'you are a very young girl. When I was your age I was wearing plaits and short white socks and I never thought about sex. You shouldn't be thinking about it.'

'It's impossible not to nowadays. It's everywhere.'

'Yes it's everywhere, but you and I don't have to make it any worse than it is already. I'll give you advice about it when you're older, not now.'

'Please, Grandma. I need to know now.'

'What's the rush?'

'Things happen very fast now.'

'Yes I know. I'm not blind.'

'Look at it like this. How many people of my age bother to go round asking adults about this kind of stuff?'

'All right Jane, if you insist. But this is just between you and me.'

'I won't tell a soul.'

'Bruce, don't do that. No! Take it outside ... Are you still there?'

'Yes.'

'Listen carefully. I'll have to speak fast because the gardener will be here any minute. Don't write it down, just remember what I say. Every girl needs to know this. Sex is for men. They're the ones who like it. These modern women who say they like it are just kidding themselves. They want to be like men but they never will be. Don't believe them. Sex is for men. You have it. They want it. That's your power. You can fool them that you enjoy it but don't fool yourself because if you do you'll start giving it away. Always strike a hard bargain and go for the best. Then you'll have a rich successful man and a rich successful life.'

'Why are women kidding themselves if they say they like it?'

'Because, my dear, at best it's a messy hit-and-miss affair. It doesn't come with a guarantee. It's for men.'

'If sex is for men, what about men who like men, and women who like women?'

'It's the same for them. The men are still men and the women are still women. Men are very simple. Women are complex and have their minds on all sorts of things. Men are the ones with the dangly things in front of them. It's on their minds all day long. It's there and all they can think about is putting it somewhere. They're really handicapped by it because it's the most important thing in their lives, and they'll do anything to keep it happy, anything. And the rest of the human beings on this planet without the dangly thing are not all that interested. If they say they are it's because they're trying to be like the ones with the dangly thing. They're not. You're not. Understand that and you'll understand life. That's all I'm saying.'

'Can I ask you one more question?'

'No.'

'Well thanks a lot, Grandma. If you change your mind let me know.'

'No, I'm not going to change my mind. Put your mother back on.'

Through the bedroom door I could see my mother's pale, worn-out face resting on her transparent bony hands as she leaned on the kitchen counter.

'She had to go out,' I said.

'Go out? Where?'

'She's gone to the cinema with a friend,' was the first thing I could come up with.

'What friend?'

36

'I don't know. She has lots of friends.'

'Since when?'

'I think it's a photographer friend of Freddy's.'

'A photographer friend?'

'Yes, he just dropped by.'

'She was talking to me five minutes ago. This friend suddenly arrived and said, "Let's go to the cinema"?'

'Yes, I think that's what happened.'

'What picture are they seeing? Why didn't you go?'

'Oh I've already seen it.'

'Seen what?'

'The film they're seeing.'

Eunice gave up, which was a good thing because if she hadn't I would have.

'Tell her to phone me.'

Conclusion: Sex is not user friendly for women as they find it difficult to concentrate on it to the degree that is required. Men have greater powers of concentration in the use of this item and therefore find it far more user friendly.

CHAPTER
7

It was like dropping a mammoth fossilised rock into my mother's lap to tell her that she had to lie about going to the movies with a photographer.

'Oh Jane,' she said painfully, 'she'll find out and then she'll be upset. Why do you do things like this?'

Freddy thought it was very funny and roared with laughter. His thick dark eyebrows with their high curving arch rose even higher as he laughed. I wondered if his fatter twin, Rumyanysev, who did so well in the Seven Years War against Prussia, used to laugh in the same manner two hundred years ago.

'Wait till the old battleaxe finds out,' he said. 'You'll have to leave the country. Both of you.' He was making himself another sandwich because I had eaten so much of the last one.

'Freddy, have you got a gun?' my mother asked, her head sinking further over the counter.

'Don't even think of shooting your mother,' he said, pressing a slice of bread on top of the sandwich which oozed out mayonnaise, tomatoes and strands of lettuce.

'Don't shoot Grandma Eunice, I'm the one who made up the story,' I said.

'Right, shoot the kid instead,' said Freddy. 'Do us all a favour.'

'No,' said my mother. 'I'm going to shoot myself.'

'Oh don't do that, please, don't leave me here with Freddy,' I pleaded.

Freddy moved his sandwich to the far end of the counter where I couldn't reach, or so he thought. 'Louise,' he said taking a big bite. 'You haven't got the wherewithal to pick a gun up, let alone shoot yourself.'

My mother looked really gloomy about that. 'Have you ever tried to commit suicide, Freddy?'

'Of course,' he said. 'Haven't we all?'

'What did you use?'

'I used Valium, Librium, a few sleeping pills, Jennifer's worm pills . . .'

'Who's Jennifer?'

'A cocker spaniel.'

'What did it feel like?'

'Terrible.'

'Really terrible?'

'Yes.'

'Hmm . . .' My mother looked as if she were seriously considering the idea. 'Why didn't it work? Didn't you take enough?'

'No,' he said, finishing off one half of the sandwich with a single bite. 'Unfortunately, I didn't have the full complement required for a successful suicide. Oh go on, Fatso.' He pushed the plate holding the rest of the sandwich down the counter to me. 'I wish you'd stop doing that starving orphan act.'

'Thanks, Freddy.' I began wolfing down the sandwich before he changed his mind.

'But if you had pulled it off,' said my mother still concentrating on the suicide, 'you wouldn't have felt a thing. It would have just been Pfft!'

'Look I just came in to make a sandwich.'

Regretfully Freddy watched me eat the last remnants of carefully mayonnaised bread and wipe the crumbs from the corner of my mouth.

'I think the best way to kill yourself is to jump off a high building,' I said. 'Because before you die you get the chance to know exactly what it feels like to go through the air in a free fall. And then you die. Crunch. That's a unique experience. That's how I'm going to kill myself.'

I slid the empty sandwich plate down the burnt, pockmarked counter top to Freddy.

'What is it with you two women?' he said disapprovingly. 'You're both talking about killing yourself. This is a really negative discussion.'

'Jane's not serious,' said my mother in the way she always makes a statement, that is, as though she's asking a question. 'She's just had a little trouble at school, that's all.'

'I haven't had trouble.' It always irritated me when she said that. 'I just don't know how to be, that's all. Whatever I am, it's always the day it's not cool to be like that.'

'Have you made out your will?' asked Freddy as he put the sandwich plate, one of his quality pieces of china, under the hot tap. The hot tap, as usual, made a deep, despairing, groaning noise as it was turned on. All the plumbing in the flat operated with noisy orchestral arrangements.

'No,' said my mother, questioningly.

Freddy sighed and shook his head. 'Don't do anything before you make out a will. You can leave everything to me. You owe me. I've been filling this refrigerator week in, week out since the day I moved in. And you two have been systematically eating everything I put in it. Your kid doesn't know the meaning of the word restraint.'

He wiped the pitted counter top carefully, several times over with a soapy J-cloth, but the counter did not change in appearance.

40

'You're a really flabby personality, Louise,' he said. 'You're sitting here toying with the idea of suicide because you haven't got the guts to face anything. This entire flat is a monument to your flabbiness. It's full of stuff you bought because you felt sorry for the salesman. It's too small. I shouldn't be living here. You should be able to afford a crappy basement like this without taking a lodger and still have plenty of cash left over at the end of the week. You're always working. Vincent doesn't pay you shit. Old Eunice is right. You shouldn't be working in a launderette. You can't say no to anyone. You'll let anyone push you around. You're a mess. You need help. There's something missing in your psyche, some gland that needs fixing. And your kid needs help too. She's going round interviewing people about sex, which is an unhealthy way to start out. She's not going to find out about sex by asking questions. She should be out there in the real world like everyone else.'

'She's not like me,' said my mother, looking very worried at the possibility, 'she's tough.'

'Of course she's tough. She has to be around a piece of wet fish like you. She's tough and she'll turn into a steam roller by the time she's fourteen. All that overcompensating will kill her.'

Freddy gave the counter one last violent rub, squeezed the J-cloth out and then went off to his room.

My mother stayed, leaning on the counter, running her fingers through her hair. I said something to her about not worrying about what people say, a standard comment I make to my mother in times of stress, but she did not take it in. She sat staring in the direction of the taps, just staring.

So I went off to pick up all the clothes and books I'd left scattered around the bedroom. Usually I could rearrange a few things and it could really distract her to see such a miracle – me engaging in an act of tidiness. But after I'd

41

performed one miraculous act and picked up all the recent things I'd left about, I had to pick up buried items that had been mulched like sodden leaves into the bedroom earth – shopping lists, old Latin tests, broken pencils, long forgotten socks and several knitted mushrooms from my knitted doll's shopping basket. I had never worked so hard to cheer her up. Usually the sight of me picking up anything could shock her out of any bad mood, but this time I went on and on, and even though I made loud clearing up noises, she did not look up once. She went on sitting at the counter and running her fingers through her hair for a long, long time.

And later, when she went to bed, she was restless, like a mouse making a nest in newspaper. It made me restless too and whenever I woke up she was rustling away. Eventually I stopped waking up, but I don't think she slept at all.

SEX 2000 – CONSUMER REPORT

Further research into the durability of virginity.

I overheard this conversation on our geography field trip. Two of the élite girls from my class, Melanie and Sibyl, were chatting at the back of the bus. I was sitting across the aisle.

'He's fourteen and he's a virgin. Personally I respect him for that,' said Sibyl.

Melanie thought about that and then asked, 'If he were sixteen what would you think?'

'I'd respect him for it.'

They both looked dubiously at each other for a moment or two.

'*Would* you?' asked Melanie.

'It is a bit old,' concluded Sibyl.

Conclusion: Under 'durability' I wrote, 'Sixteen too old'.

CHAPTER

8

I eventually told Sophia about the boy.

'He's going to work for Vincent on Saturdays,' I told her. 'He has an earring but it's held in place by a magnet.'

It was an obvious sign that his parents wouldn't let him get his ears pierced.

'Oh,' groaned Sophia, 'not exactly a hard lad. On the other hand he'll be easy to handle. If he has a magnet it means he does what his parents tell him. In which case he'll do what you tell him.'

'I'm not going to tell him to do anything,' I said. 'I don't have an agenda of things I need done.'

'How old is he?'

'About fourteen.'

'And what's his name?'

'Garvie.'

'Makes a change from Nick.'

In the late seventies and early eighties a large proportion of mothers in the London area decided to call their baby sons Nicholas, and by the nineties there was hardly a school girl in the metropolis who did not claim to have at least one boyfriend called Nick.

Garvie had brown hair flopping in his eyes which he shook back like a terrier getting out of a lake. He was ordinary looking, but I was ready to put up with almost anything. Even the magnet, which was pretty pathetic.

The thing that I found wildly attractive about him was that he was a boy, a truly plus factor as far as I was concerned. Once again let me remind you that I wash my hands entirely of the extremely naïve child I was; I'm reporting historical events that took place several lifetimes ago. I am not that person. I am larger, older, different. She is nothing to me except as a tale to be told.

At that time, she, or I as I was, lacked knowledge of young males on many levels. There were none of them in my school, I did not have a brother and I did not meet many males, in the younger category, in the course of an average day. Males like Freddy and Vincent did not count as they were severely blunted by age.

Apart from his obvious advantage of being a boy there was not much else to recommend Garvie. I found out from Vincent's girlfriend, Dolores, that he lived in Barnes and that he cycled to work without a crash helmet. His job consisted of running errands for Vincent, i.e. buying him ham and cheese rolls, washing cars, and telling him when Dolores was coming up the alley.

'You can tell him about your research,' said Sophia on the phone, 'and ask him to help you out – sexually speaking.'

I was horrified. 'Sophia, give me a break. I haven't even got him to look in my direction yet. He doesn't know I exist. It'll be years before I speak to him.'

'You'd better hurry up,' said Sophia, sounding bored. 'Experience is really important.'

'I don't want experience.'

'You have to have it. After the summer term you'll only have four more years in school. That's not all that long. You'll feel like a real dork if you haven't done it by the time you're doing your A-levels. Nobody will speak to you.'

'Then I'll do it the day before my last A-level. I'll hold my nose and plunge in.'

'It's not a cough medicine. You're supposed to like it.'

It was all very well for her to say. Life was simple for Sophia. She had her own private line so there was no problem with her parents getting angry about talking too long on the phone. I always had Freddy nagging me about keeping the line clear for his agent so I would have to continue this discussion in furtive notes passed across the classroom.

I could imagine Sophia stretched across her Navaho blanket on her Chiswick pine bed, surrounded by her teddy bears, and studying for the all encompassing physics test we were to have on Monday morning. I longed for everything to be like the physics test. You studied for it, you were tested, and you either got it right or wrong.

SEX 2000 - CONSUMER REPORT

How vital is sex?

I asked my mother about this because I had to get some data and there was no one else to interview.

'Did you find life when you found sex?' I asked, when she was doing the washing up.

'Life?' My mother looked extremely puzzled. 'How do you mean *find life?*'

'You know – life. Like the meaning of life. Did you think you were closer to it?'

'After having sex?'

'Yes.'

'No.'

'Not even a smidgen nearer?' I asked disappointedly.

'Not the smallest smidgen.'

VICKERY TURNER

'What did you find then?'

'A lot of panting. A lot of rolling about.'

'Was it fun?'

'Fun. I suppose it might have been. It was such a long time ago.'

'Do you think you didn't find life in sex because you didn't look hard enough?'

'How hard do you have to look?'

'I don't know. It's no good asking me. I'm only thirteen and backward for my years.'

'I was a romantic,' said my mother with a note of despair. 'A look in someone's eye. Something they said. My mind wasn't below the belt.'

'So if they changed the rule and said sex wasn't rolling about and panting any more but instead it was going to be ... just rubbing noses and nothing else ... would you be annoyed that they'd changed it?'

'Not in the slightest.'

'That probably means you're undersexed.'

'Good. I don't care,' my mother said emphatically.

Conclusion: Under 'value' I wrote, 'Not fully appreciated by all members of the public'.

CHAPTER
9

A thick, grey cloud hung over the rooftops on Saturday morning and the workmen on the railway bridge that connected the borough of Hammersmith and Fulham to the borough of Kensington and Chelsea were moving mysteriously behind the high green boards they had set up. Someone, perhaps an angry motorist who wanted to get his bridge back, had splashed the words WE NEVER RUSH in white paint on one of the green boards. The bridge had been out of service for over three months and Freddy was threatening to chain himself to the parapet if they did not finish it soon.

Bridge life had become more squashed than ever after a policeman's horse had left a generous supply of manure on the narrow footpath that led to the leafy avenues of Holland Park, and pedestrians had to tiptoe carefully. Perhaps it was a plot by the Borough of Kensington and Chelsea to keep us undesirables out of their district.

I went off to Vincent's with my mother because I was hoping to get another glimpse of Garvie. In order to get this glimpse I had agreed to be exploited child labour in the gruesome launderette, for hardly any money.

I didn't worry about the minuscule wages nearly as much as the shiny pink nylon overall I had to wear. My mother said it made me look like a strawberry milkshake but I thought it made me look like a jar of pink slime. And if that was not bad enough the day turned out to be THE DAY, the beginning of a process in which I, step by step, went from being the child of a single parent to being almost an orphan. I gave my mother away, body and soul. That is to say, my mother's body and soul were presented on a plate to a man who didn't want them. And it was all my fault.

It seemed like a normal Saturday. The workmen on the site at the end of Vincent's alley were as rude as usual. I was going to say something rude back but my mother dragged me past.

'But he asked if I wanted his dick. That's not polite,' I protested. 'He shouldn't get away with that.'

'There's nothing you can do,' my mother whispered. 'If you say anything, they'll see it as an invitation. They'll think you're a trollop.'

'That's not fair. There must be something you can say. I'll work on it.'

'Don't,' said my mother.

The first thing we noticed as we walked up the alley was Vincent's girlfriend, Dolores. She was behind the counter in the reception office in her Levi 501s and high-heeled boots, several gold chains, and three earrings in each ear. She was a hairdresser and made liberal use of hair products. The powerful scent of her shampoo, conditioner, mousse and spray bombe assaulted us as we opened the door.

Dolores was obviously getting bored with other people's hair. She had recently taken to making occasional assaults on Vincent's Coachworks and throwing her weight around. She'd had her eyes set on the office for some time and now here she was, sitting in my mother's chair, giving the appearance of being busy. To do this she was raising her eyebrows, looking up and down the office, up and down, and making exasperated sighing noises.

'You should see the pile of service washes in there.' She pointed in the direction of the launderette. 'Be a love and get started and I'll hold the fort here.'

My mother looked upset but, of course, didn't say anything. Any other human being would have said something, but my mother was not in the normal category of human beings. To leave Dolores in complete charge of the office for an entire Saturday was a really daft idea. She made a shambles of the files whenever she went near them. They were not a priority for her. What was important was the decor. I could see that she had already put lace covers around the Kleenex box and paper flowers on the counter; they looked really silly among the grimy bits of old cars. My mother gave one last heartbroken glance towards the filing cabinets and then dragged herself away to the launderette.

'Tell her to get out of your office,' I whispered to my mother. 'She doesn't know what to do. And if she gets something wrong Vincent'll blame you.'

'I know,' said my mother, but she didn't say anything. She had only one way of handling Dolores, and that was to wait for her to go away. That's how she dealt with all flashy, insensitive people. That's how she dealt with my father. She waited for him to go away, and he did.

Halfway through the morning, after we'd done too many service washes, too many socks and shirts and knickers, and we were almost flat on our backs with exhaustion, Dolores wafted into the launderette holding a bag of washing at arm's length to prevent contamination.

'Customer outside. Paying for his car. Says he'll wait if you do it fast.' And she rushed off, tottering slightly on the uneven, pot-holed linoleum.

There were no machines available so the bag was placed

with all the other prospective service washes. When Dr Arnold Jefferies turned up five minutes later my mother and I realised with horror that the newly arrived bag was his. It was, of course, his day to collect his Ford Escort XRI.

He walked in, via the back door, with the expression of one who fully expected his laundry to be already dry and folded. He gazed at his bag with the disturbing certainty of one who thought five minutes was ample time to wash, dry and fold his laundry. I was just about to explain the limitations of time regarding service washes when Vincent arrived.

During the week Dr Jefferies had appeared on breakfast television and Vincent had come to congratulate him; it seemed that he had already congratulated his celebrity customer outside in the alley but obviously did not want to let the enjoyment of it and the contact high slip away too quickly. He began digging his chin into Dr Jefferies' shoulder like the Duchess in *Alice in Wonderland*. He was very star struck.

If Dr Jefferies paid any attention at all to Vincent it was only as one looking at an annoying fly, he was fully occupied with staring expectantly at his bag of washing. Vincent saw it as an opportunity.

'Is that yours?' he asked. No sooner had Dr Jefferies nodded than Vincent grabbed the washing and threw it at my mother. 'Do that pronto. And don't lose any socks for God's sake.'

My mother caught the bag, staggered back a few steps, fell against a washing machine and winced with pain as the sharp corner jabbed her between the shoulder blades. She tried to look cheerful about it. I felt like screaming and saying, 'Complain for God's sake!' But I didn't because I knew it would just make her die a little bit more. And then I would have to die a little bit with her. It wasn't worth it.

We had a small piece of luck after that. Two washing machines finished their cycles simultaneously. So we separated the colours from the whites and put them in the two machines for a warm wash while Dr Jefferies tried to find a seat without a ripped plastic cover and studied some papers from his briefcase. He looked out of place, scholarly and important but his washing let him down. His underwear had quite a few holes and some of his shirts had frayed cuffs.

'I think he can afford better underwear,' whispered my mother, 'but he probably can't be bothered to go and buy it.'

He didn't look like a launderette type of person, especially this launderette with its dank, dark walls that peeled like petticoats, layer upon layer. He looked around the place suspiciously; his neck and head remained stiff while his eyes were moving to left and right, examining the ragged customers, the chipped walls and the notice stating 'The Management cannot take responsibility for lost items'.

Vincent, in a red tartan shirt and oil-stained jeans, hovered around looking for an excuse not to leave. It was not often that he had a television star in his peeling green launderette and he needed an opportunity to show off in front of him.

'So this is your first time in a launderette eh?' he asked Dr Jefferies. 'Makes a change from being on TV all the time.' He gave a big belly laugh as though he'd just made a brilliantly witty joke and his skinny red pony tail rattled and shook.

Dr Jefferies, quite rightly, thought it was a dumb remark and hardly looked up from his papers. So then Vincent started looking for some other way to make an impression. I could see his eyes darting from one customer's face to another, searching for something that would entertain the visitor but all the customers were hardly breathing, hunched over their washing machines searching for life in their whirling suds. The only one who was in any kind of motion was a woman searching for her socks which had disappeared mysteriously during a service wash. He began studying her hopefully.

The woman was saying accusingly to my mother, 'My daughter knitted those socks. They're the last socks she'll ever knit because where she's going they're not allowed knitting needles.'

Vincent tucked in his tartan shirt and whirred into motion. 'Don't you realise,' he screamed at my mother, loud enough to wake most of the lifeless customers, 'that these socks are family mementos. That girl will never knit a sock again. They are irreplaceable!'

At that moment Dolores returned along the echoing corridor that connected the launderette to the alley, her heels tapping bossily on the cement floor. She tottered in with a pile of blankets and dropped them by the door. 'Rush job,' she said and tottered off.

Vincent pointed to the blankets and yelled at my mother, 'Get your arse over there. It's a rush job.'

I think I had the only mother in the whole of Greater London who could not tell Vincent to stick it in his ear, or words to that effect. I had the only mother who couldn't figure out what to do, she didn't know whether to look for the socks or what. She froze. And whenever my mother froze Vincent went on and on shouting at her; it happened quite often and they would get like two wind-up dolls stuck in one action.

Vincent eventually took a break from shouting and went over to Dr Jefferies. 'She drives me crazy,' he said pointing to my mother, who immediately turned her back towards Vincent and became very absorbed in a carton of soap powder.

Dr Jefferies frowned, put down the paper he was reading

and studied my mother's back in the same intense manner that she was studying the soap powder. 'Abnormally low domination personality,' he said. 'Alice was like that but she got eaten.'

My mother was close enough to hear. If she'd been a dog her ears would have stuck up in the air but nothing happened except that her face went a raspberry colour, as usual, and she slunk out to the store room in the pretence of getting more soap.

Shortly after that Dr Jefferies gave up waiting for his washing and went home. I think he would have liked to have taken it home with him but it was quite obvious that he grew heartily sick of Vincent breathing down his neck. He said he would pick it up later and Vincent said not to bother, his delivery service would bring it to his door.

'Louise!' he yelled. 'Deliver Dr Jefferies' washing the minute it's ready. OK? No farting about.'

My mother, whose face had temporarily closed down and was not registering expressions, mumbled that yes she would. As he walked out of the door Dr Jefferies threw a curious, probing glance at my mother, not unlike the look he gave his cageful of rats when he pulled them out of his car. My mother felt it and ducked behind a washing machine.

I could not worry about my mother for an entire Saturday. Life was passing me by. I was stuck in the launderette and Garvie was working outside in the alley, and I was not going to get an opportunity to speak to him unless I made one. I went up to the office and suggested to Dolores that I swept the area outside the office door and she thought it was a brilliant idea; she would have liked artificial turf and a striped awning, but sweeping was a start. There was not a large area to sweep because of Vincent's auto bric-a-brac lining the walls on both sides of the alley but there was a patch.

I managed to stay out in the alley running a broom over the strip of cobblestones for about forty-five minutes before I even caught sight of Garvie. He was walking from one side of the alley where they do the respraying to the other side, that's to say, the lavatories. He was there for two minutes. As soon as he emerged I clattered my broom against the cobblestones and swept vigorously. He stopped and looked to see what on earth the noise was and I gave a performance of wildly energetic sweeping. He went on his way but I was extremely pleased with the results. I had made contact. A boy knew I existed.

SEX 2000 – CONSUMER REPORT

Further research on the value of sex.

When I took the rush-job blankets up to the office I explained to Dolores that I was having a difficult time finding people for my survey and she was surprisingly sympathetic. She agreed, on the spot, to an interview. What a coup!

'I have a little experience in that area,' she told me. 'What do you want to know?'

'How valuable is sex?' I asked.

'I'd say it's about the most important thing in your life,' she said with relish. 'You can't underestimate the value of a good sex life.'

Tragically, at that point, a customer came into the office and we had to stop there.

Conclusion: Under 'value' I wrote, 'some members of the public find it extremely valuable. More details later.'

CHAPTER
10

We were late setting out to deliver Dr Jefferies' washing because the work had piled up and we couldn't get away. According to Vincent we had to return by two-thirty which was humanly impossible and my mother's fingers were trembling as she turned the ignition key.

I tried to calm her down. 'So what if Vincent gets mad? So what? Does the world come to an end?'

'I'm tired of being yelled at. I've had enough for one day.'

She chewed her lower lip and pulled out carefully into the traffic as if she were in charge of a huge container lorry.

'Don't worry. Vincent's all bark,' I said.

'It's the bark I don't like.'

As we headed towards Shepherd's Bush Green I said, 'I'm going to interview him for Sex 2000. He's agreed but it's hard to catch him.'

My mother frowned. 'I think you should give up this sex survey, Jane. Have a childhood for a little longer. Why don't you go back to doing Travel 2000? You shouldn't be talking to people like Vincent, of all people, and asking him about his sex life. He's too jaded and you're just too young. Everybody lies anyway.'

'But I've put in all this work, you can't expect me to go back. I don't want to do travel. It's boring. And anyway I'm not too young. Have you been under a rock? When you get to thirteen, all you talk about is boys.'

'You talk about boys, yes. But that's not sex. I talked about boys when I was thirteen. It was just kids' stuff.'

'It's not anymore Sophia has almost done it three times now. She said people go on about it so much she'll be grateful when she can get it out of the way and have some peace. And now she's nagging me about doing it.'

'That's Sophia. Sophia has a few problems.'

'Not really. We're all the same. We're all talking about sex. We dream about it.'

'You dream about it!'

'Of course. Didn't you?'

'No I didn't. How could I? I didn't know anything about it.'

'I dream about it.'

'Dream what?'

'All my friends dream the same thing. They dream they're having sex.'

'Is it realistic?'

'No, it's a dream.'

'How can you dream about something you don't know anything about?'

'You see it on television all the time, on videos – it's impossible to avoid.'

'Oh God! I think that's terrible. What's happening to the world? When I was thirteen I dreamed about bicycles and trips to the seaside.'

'I dream about bicycles.'

'They've taken over dreams. They've stolen your child-hood. They're stealing our children.'

'Don't be so dramatic.'

'I can't help it. I think it's awful.'

'Where are you going?'

My mother had just turned the corner to go round Shepherd's Bush Green for the second time. 'Oh I don't know. Where am I going? I'm so depressed that you're having those dreams, Jane.'

'Everyone in my class does.'

'Everyone?'

'Well, I haven't carried out a survey.'

'Oh God. It's like the Invasion of the Bodysnatchers. You've been taken over. Our children's dreams are being taken over. They're not safe, even when we tuck them up in bed. Oh God, I hate sex!'

For the second time we circled Shepherd's Bush Green, which was its usual worn, not very green self. Every blade of grass on the green was impregnated with dust and carbon monoxide and trodden underfoot by too many boots and paws per square inch. We headed for Holland Park where the grass retained more of its natural juices and found Dr Jefferies' house. We were, by then, almost an hour behind schedule.

Dr Jefferies' house was one of the more shabby, overgrown houses in an impressive row of perfect, white buildings with white columns and graceful balconies. His columns were gently decaying and his balcony drooped, but he was at the end and, being this far removed, obviously felt no pressure to keep up with his neighbours.

My mother found a parking space outside his door where we had a clear view of a window box of dying plants and a dull brass door knocker.

'Get his washing off the back seat and take it in. I'll wait here,' said my mother.

'I'm not taking it in. You take it in,' I said.

'What's wrong? Why won't you take it in?' She looked panicked.

'Because I don't want to. You deliver it. It's your job.'

'Come on, Jane. It won't cost you anything just to go up to that door and hand the washing in.'

'How do you know if it will cost me anything? Maybe I'm not a bulldozer. Maybe I'm very sensitive.'

My mother's hands were gripping the steering wheel very tightly. 'I know you're sensitive, but you're not that sensitive. All you have to do is deliver the washing for goodness sake. Is that such a big deal?'

'If it's such a small thing, why don't you do it?'

'How can I go up to that door when he said I was like one of his rats?'

'He's forgotten about that. You can tell he doesn't remember anything personal like that.'

'Jane, please, I'm begging you.'

'You're wasting your time.'

'What kind of friend are you?'

'I don't have to be your friend. There's no law.'

'Then simply out of human decency, will you take that washing up to that door and let's get out of here? I'm over an hour late and Vincent's going to make my life hell. Do you want that?'

'No, I don't want it. I think you should tell Vincent to stop making your life hell.'

'Please, Jane.'

'I'll go if you come with me.' It was my first and final offer.

'Don't be silly. You don't need a deputation to deliver one bag of washing. Please, Jane. Just do it and let's go.'

'I can't.'

'Well I'm not going to do it.'

My mother slumped her head on the steering wheel and accidentally hit the horn. The small, plaintive hoot sounded larger and louder than ever before, in fact much louder.

'Aaagh!' My mother was horrified and wrenched herself

upright. She was rigid with consternation.

A face appeared at the ground-floor window of Dr Jefferies' house, disappeared and then a couple of seconds later the front door opened. A woman with grey hair styled in a 'forties roll, an apron over a stout body, and carpet slippers came down the front path towards our car.

'Yes?' she asked.

'We've brought Dr Jefferies' washing,' my mother said in a breathy voice.

'Oh good,' the woman turned and went back towards the house. 'Bring it in. They're fixing the washing machine now but he needs a new one. I keep on telling him, go to John Lewis and get a new one, but he won't listen.'

My mother suddenly came alive. She bounced out of the driver's seat, dragged Dr Jefferies' washing off the back seat and ran up to the front door.

'Here it is!' she said, thrusting the washing under the woman's nose.

The women shook her head and waved it away. 'Bring it in. It's too heavy for me.'

By this time I was behind my mother and she turned and pushed the bag of washing at me. I pushed it back at her. This went on several times with the pushing getting more violent each time.

The woman turned to investigate the small gasps and scuffling noise going on behind her and like small children playing pass-the-parcel, we stopped immediately. My mother was left holding the bag.

'Come in,' said the woman.

My mother stepped cautiously inside the front doorway as if she were checking a field for a mad bull. She dropped the bag inside the door and backed out with rare speed.

'Please,' insisted the woman, 'could you bring it into the kitchen?'

We followed her capacious rear across an entrance hall that was lined with books, floor to ceiling, presided over by the bust of an ancient Greek on a rickety plinth. It seemed like the sort of professor's house you'd find in a comic strip.

At the end of the hall was the kitchen where a workman was on his hands and knees, looking at a washing machine that was tipped against a wall. The woman pointed to a table and my mother dropped the bag on it and backed away as quickly as she could. But I was not so anxious to leave now I'd made it past the front door and I paused to have a look around the kitchen. And my pausing there and then was probably one more nail in my mother's coffin. Maybe the whole thing would never have happened if I had followed her out quickly. I make no excuses for myself. I was a pernicious little twit in those days.

So there was I having a good look around just because I wanted to see what the kitchen looked like. There was not much to see, unfortunately. It was a plain white, rather boring kitchen, which had a strong smell of pine disinfectant.

The woman lowered herself slowly on to a chair, dropping into a free fall for the last couple of inches, and watched the workman; then she looked up at me. 'How old are you?' she asked.

'Thirteen.'

'My granddaughter is thirteen. She's good at athletics. She loves to run.' She looked at me critically, as if the fact that I didn't look like a runner was a real minus factor.

A muffled crash came from the floor above us. The woman rolled her eyes, 'I knew that would happen.' She pointed up to the ceiling. 'You know what he should do? He should write a book on self-control.'

The washing machine repair man and I both looked up as though we expected an explanation for her remark to be written on the ceiling.

'Mrs Moon!' yelled a nasty, bad-tempered voice from upstairs.

'There he goes,' said Mrs Moon knowingly, but she remained in her chair.

On the refrigerator was a poster advertising *The Killer Instinct and You*, held in place by four ceramic frogs. 'Learn this killer instinct, overcome lifelong fear and be a success for the first time in your life,' claimed the ad.

'Is that true?' I pointed to the poster.

Mrs Moon turned her eyes slowly to the poster and looked at it distrustfully. 'It's true if you're a rat.'

'Have you read it?' I asked. 'Do you think it would help my mother?'

'No I haven't read it.'

'Could my mother get a few tips from that book? Her boss is really abusive.'

'Mrs Moon!' screamed the voice upstairs.

'If you want abusive, he's your man for the job.' She rolled her eyes again. 'He's the most abusive man you'd ever want to meet.'

'Jane,' my mother said, putting her head round the kitchen door. 'Let's go. We're late.'

'Nice meeting you,' I said to Mrs Moon and the workman, and I went out into the hall where my mother was glowering with annoyance.

'You didn't have to talk about me,' she whispered.

'I thought she might give me a free copy of his book,' I whispered back.

My mother headed for the front door, tiptoeing for some reason, but before she could get halfway across the hall, a door at the top of the stairs flew open and a man's voice yelled harshly, 'Mrs Moon, what the hell have you been doing here?'

A wild-eyed Dr Arnold Jefferies came storming down the

stairs and came face to face with my mother.

'Aaagh!' he backed away in distaste rather than surprise, distaste at being confronted by a woman in a pink overall at the bottom of his stairs.

My mother did not say anything. She was transfixed and her face, which was always a problem, had an expression of sheer horror on it.

Dr Jefferies examined this face scientifically, dissecting it piece by piece, and came to his conclusion. 'Haven't we met somewhere before?' he asked. 'Was it at the symposium last week?'

VINCENT'S LAUNDERETTE – embroidered on my mother's pocket in bright red silk by Dolores – flashed at him like a neon sign.

'No,' said my mother with the voice of a minnow. 'It was at the launderette this morning.'

'Ah,' he said and walked past her and went on his way to the kitchen.

'Let's go!' I said to my mother, but she wouldn't move. I think she was either glued to the floor or she felt that now it was impolite to rush off after having had a conversation.

We watched Dr Jefferies lean over the half-tipped washing machine and the legs of the repairman and snarl at Mrs Moon. 'What the hell have you been doing in my study? Didn't I tell you not to touch anything?'

Through the doorway we could see Mrs Moon staring back at him with cold, codfish eyes, obviously unimpressed. I could see that the workman made a quick decision to keep out of it and he went on tapping the washing machine even though Dr Jefferies was yelling in his ear.

'I didn't move anything important,' said Mrs Moon.

'You moved notes!'

'You don't write notes on Mars bar wrappers.'

He did not accept this allegation. The two of them stared

aggressively at each other like two seasoned wrestlers, then Dr Jefferies exhaled a lot of angry air, turned furiously back to the stairs and bumped into my mother again.

I was standing by the front door trying to encourage her to move but she would not. My mother told me afterwards that she had remained in the hall, standing as still as the Greek bust next to her, out of politeness. She was always doing things to be polite. She was so polite that she ended up doing impolite, intrusive things like hanging around to eavesdrop on Dr Jefferies' confrontation with Mrs Moon.

Dr Jefferies blinked, trying to figure out who she was. I thought he was going to ask her all over again if they had met at the symposium last week. But then daylight dawned as he cleverly decided to read the words embroidered in bright red on her pocket.

'Right, the launderette,' he said. A flicker of interest came into his eyes. Perhaps he recalled that here was the low domination personality who was like the rat who got eaten.

Mrs Moon leaned out of her chair and yelled across the washing machine repairman's back, 'This young lady wants to talk to you about the killer instinct because her boss is abusive.'

She hurled the remark down the hall, possibly to annoy him, it was hard to tell without knowing her a little better. But whatever her intention, it certainly did annoy him.

There was a deadly silence while he looked at several books in his bookcase, then he looked at his feet and then he looked up at my mother. He was doing something funny with his teeth, which was going on behind a closed mouth. I think he was bouncing his top front teeth onto the lower ones, which meant he had to jut his jaw forward.

My mother's shoulders had frozen en route to her ears, stopping halfway. And Dr Jefferies started to read the lettering on my mother's overall again. So I came forward and said, 'My mother needs a few tips.'

Obviously this was the wrong thing to say. Academics and scientists get very huffy if you don't treat them with respect and say the right thing. I think it's because they lack charm and if they don't get respect they'll get no attention at all.

Dr Jefferies said quietly, 'I don't give tips. It's a science.'

'Oh,' I said.

My mother started to move. She grabbed my arm and tried to pull me towards the front door.

'It's a science,' repeated Dr Jefferies. 'Science has laws, rules. You follow them one by one. Action, reaction. You study. You practise. It's all law. I don't have any tips.'

'OK. Sorry to bother you,' I said.

He started walking up the stairs. He was not the type to end conversations neatly.

And I turned to follow my mother out of the door.

That's when it happened.

My mother, who by now wanted to get away so badly, was held up once again. But this time it was not because of an excess of politeness.

She simply could not move. She started to tremble and tears came to her eyes. And then more tears in a steady conveyer belt down to her chin. She started sobbing. Little sobs first. Then she began to gasp for air and she sounded as if she were going to choke.

The man fixing the washing machine gave up trying to be uninvolved and put his head around the kitchen door to see what on earth was going on. He was on all fours so he looked like a curious dog. Mrs Moon pulled herself out of her chair and came out into the hall. And Dr Jefferies stopped walking up the stairs and turned.

My mother, whose only aim in life was to be avoid getting looked at, was the centre of attention.

The choking seemed to go on for ever, though it probably

64

wasn't all that long. As soon as my mother regained some control over herself she started saying, 'I'm sorry. I'm sorry.'

Dr Jefferies stood halfway up the stairs with his leg poised in the air like a discus thrower. He watched my mother with a mixture of disgust and fascination as if she were a bad traffic accident. The washing machine man remained on all fours peering round the door post.

Only Mrs Moon had any gumption. She took my mother down the hall to a small room, book-lined floor-to-ceiling like the hall, but also containing a large brown and white check sofa into whose welcoming softness Mrs Moon pushed my mother. She stood guard over her and sent me to the kitchen to get her a glass of water.

The washing machine man looked at me warily when I went into the kitchen. 'What's she on then?' he asked.

'I couldn't begin to tell you,' I said, and left quickly.

For a long time my mother couldn't hold the glass of water because she was shaking so much but Mrs Moon held the glass to her lips and made her take a sip. That way she eventually gulped down the whole glassful.

'What's the trouble, dear?' Mrs Moon asked.

My mother couldn't answer.

So I said, 'She's upset because we're late.'

My mother wobbled her head to indicate disagreement and emitted the half-choked, barely audible words: 'No I'm not.'

'What is it then?' I asked.

'I'm terribly sorry,' she was still gulping and gasping. 'We'd better go now.'

She stood up but her knees buckled and she sat down again. 'Sorry,' she apologised to the sofa.

Mrs Moon, although overweight and a little on the old side, had the remnants of an attractive face on which she had put eyeliner and mascara. She made my mother a cup of tea and gave me a lemonade. Although there were two leather armchairs in the room, the three of us crowded together on to the sofa in an act of solidarity.

'Don't worry about being late,' said Mrs Moon. 'Tell him the car broke down.'

'She can't lie. It shows on her face,' I said.

Mrs Moon examined my mother's tear-soaked cheeks and appeared discouraged by what she saw. She shook her head sadly and said, 'You're in a bad way.'

And that was it, really. We left as soon as my mother's knees stopped buckling when she stood up.

Mrs Moon waved us goodbye and we drove through winding streets, past the high hedges of graceful communal gardens with privileged pathways and banks of hidden flowers, looking for a way out. The one-way streets, which were there to keep outsiders off the secluded avenues, served to keep us locked in a maze. We went blindly from one isolated street to another with not one kindly pedestrian to advise us. It seemed that few souls felt worthy to venture among these urban palaces with their calm interiors.

My mother, still gulping back the occasional sob, slowly found her way out on to the Bayswater Road and then back to the familiar solace of Shepherd's Bush roundabout. The ball had started rolling for my mother. At that point there was still time to stop the whole thing, turn it around. But I didn't, my mother didn't. Neither of us had any idea that it would turn out so – well – explosively.

Good fortune smiled on us when we drove back down the alley to Vincent's because he was too busy with a tricky piece of respraying to notice our return. Dolores remarked that my mother looked 'poorly' and she said if Vincent asked, she would tell him we'd been back hours.

The icing on the cake was that Garvie had to bring a crate of bleach into the launderette. He dropped it in the storage room and when he came out he walked right by me. He was not more than a metre away and I could see a mole on his neck. *Formidable*! It was debatable whether or not he looked at me. But I was sure that we were now within a hair's breadth of actually speaking to each other. As it was, I almost said, 'The bleach doesn't go there,' but thought better of it. I didn't want to put him off.

SEX 2000 – CONSUMER REPORT

Why is sex the most important thing in our life?

While my mother was mopping the floor in the launderette, I cornered Dolores just as she was locking the office door. She agreed to a five-minute interview.

'You said sex is the most important thing in our life. Could you go into more detail?' I asked her. 'For instance what has sex done for you?'

'It's given me excitement, good times, it's made me what I am,' answered Dolores. 'It got me Vincent.'

'It got you Vincent. Is that good? Was it worthwhile?'

She thought about that and did not come up with an answer. So I had to prod. 'Did you like Vincent when you first met him?'

'No.'

'So why did you choose him?'

Dolores thought about that. 'I used to get all hot when I was around Vincent. When I first met him.'

'Hot – what do you mean? Could you go into more detail?'

Dolores gave me a disparaging look. 'You know,' she said, 'stirred up.'

'Could you describe it?'

'Hot, you feel all hot. One minute the guy's looking ugly and you wouldn't touch him with a bargepole, then you get this hot feeling and all of a sudden he's Mel Gibson.'

'The hot feeling made *Vincent* look like Mel Gibson?' I asked disbelievingly.

'Yes,' said Dolores, possibly with a tinge of regret.

'The hot feeling wasn't telling you the truth. When you cooled down, did you wish you hadn't listened to it?'

I received a second disparaging look from Dolores. 'I wasn't listening to anything. It was a feeling. It wasn't talking to me. It didn't have a voice.'

'Well then, let me get this straight just for the record. You get all hot, then you start imagining things about someone, and then what?'

'You get together.'

'Is that good?'

Dolores looked irritated by the question. 'Is that good? What does *that* mean? It can be good. Sometimes it is, sometimes it isn't. It depends how it turns out afterwards, really.'

'How did it turn out for you and Vincent?'

Dolores stared at me blankly. 'Well I'm here aren't I?'

'So the sequence was, you felt hot, he looked like Mel Gibson, you got together, and now you've ended up here.'

We both looked up the dark alley which was looking particularly grubby and cluttered. Dolores sighed.

'If someone had come up to you,' I asked, 'before you met Vincent, and said you'd end up here, what would you have said?'

'I'd have punched them on the nose.'

'Why didn't you punch Vincent on the nose?'

'Because there he was, sitting in this pub, looking all sexy. And I got an urge I couldn't control.'

'Why couldn't you control it?'

'I don't know.'

'Did you ever try to control it?'

'I didn't want to.'

'If you'd wanted to, do you think you could have controlled it?'

'Maybe. I don't know.'

'If you'd known about ending up in the alley do you think you could have controlled it?'

'It's too late to ask me that now. I mean, I'll say this for Vincent, I'll give him A for effort. He's not a sex machine, but who is? London pubs are full of lousy lovers.'

'How do you know?'

Dolores looked shifty. 'It's common knowledge.'

'So how good is Vincent?'

'I'd give him a three.'

'Out of ten?'

'Yes.'

'If you could choose between making Vincent a ten or turning this alley into a ten, which would you have?'

'How do you mean turn this alley into a ten?'

'Like turning it into a Rolls Royce showroom in Mayfair or turning Vincent into the most amazing lover ever.'

'Well, there's no choice is there? It's obvious.'

'You'd choose the amazing lover?'

'Don't be daft. I've got to go now, love.'

Dolores trotted away down the cobblestones.

Conclusion: (1) Sex cannot be relied on to help us see clearly, as it can make ugly, bad-tempered people seem better looking and friendly. (2) Although some members of the public find sex extremely valuable its by-products can disappoint the consumer.

CHAPTER

11

Freddy had spilt the beans. In a rare moment of chattering on the phone to Eunice, he told her that my mother had been 'taken ill' while out delivering washing.

To Eunice's ears 'delivering washing' was more of an alarming term than 'taken ill', but it was a major misfortune that she heard either. It was the result of my not getting to the phone quickly enough. Whenever it rang I went for it in a headlong tackle and tried to catch it before the first ring was over but Freddy, assuming that it was his agent, always flew through the air and fell on it before I could get there.

'You'd move faster if you were an actor,' he used to say.

So he pounced on the phone, which was the first piece of bad luck and the second was that he was in a good mood. Usually, when he found out that it was not his agent but my grandmother, he would say 'Oh,' like someone who'd trodden on a slug. But this time he was saying things like, 'How are you, Eunice?' and then before he could be stopped he was telling her all about the breakdown.

My mother and I were both very angry with Freddy.

'Now what have I done wrong?' he moaned.

'You've blabbed to Grandma Eunice,' I said very resentfully.

'Oh, Freddy,' my mother said sadly.

70

'So shoot me,' he said. 'I was being friendly to an old lady. What's so terrible about that?'

'Freddy, you know what she does with information. You never let her have information.'

'It's about time,' he said huffily, 'that you people got a little more normal. Communicating, making conversation is what people do on this planet. That's why we have telephones.'

So the cat was out of the bag and my mother was ordered to meet Eunice somewhere on neutral ground the following Saturday. She could not go, of course, because Vincent would not let her have any time off, so I was sent in her place.

We met in the courtyard café at St James Church, Piccadilly, and had tea and carrot cake surrounded by pigeons and starlings. To my surprise my father had been summoned too, and he did not appear all that excited about it, especially after a pigeon splattered on his Valentino suit. I was immediately dispatched to get a glass of water and some napkins to wash it off.

Whenever I met my father he would say that he was happy to see me, but if I spoke to him it would take some time for him to register what I had said. I felt that my face was a television screen transmitting a football match that kept him distracted. He could move the television screen at will. Throughout the tea he moved it from my face to Eunice's, to a pigeon and on to a teapot. He was watching the match the whole time and only half concentrating on us.

In appearance my father was not unlike the man in the white suit instructing the ballet dancers in Degas' 'Le Foyer de Danse à l'Opera', a picture very familiar to me because it was on the cover of my Impressionists address and telephone book. My father looked like that man except that he

71

combed his hair back more sleekly and had a smaller moustache. But he had the same receding hairline and identical nose, jawline and cheeks.

While I was away getting the glass of water and napkins to clean my father's suit, a plot was hatched. When I came back, Eunice said, in a careful voice, 'Jane, we're going to get your mother some psychiatric help.'

My father wiped his suit with wet napkins and nodded in agreement. 'Your mother needs help.'

'What sort of psychiatric help.' I asked, thinking of the things they did to Sylvia Plath, as described in *The Bell Jar* – electric shocks and other such horrors.

Eunice patted her hair into place. 'We'll have to shop around.'

'Have you heard of Dr Arnold Jefferies?' I asked.

'Who's he?'

'An American.'

'An American?' My father's lip curled in distaste.

'He's one of the launderette customers,' Eunice explained to him. 'It was his house she broke down in.'

'Oh.' My father's lip curled still further.

'He says he can teach anyone the killer instinct,' I said.

'That's the kind of thing an American would say,' replied my father. 'Your mother needs real help, not phoney baloney.'

They changed the subject and Richard told Eunice about his plans to become a Member of Parliament. They were vague plans but he had started by becoming a school governor, and seemed pleased about that. The discussion drew my father completely away from the football match he'd been watching on his movable screen. He felt that getting back with my mother, even if it was 'only for official occasions to start off with', would be a good career move as family was important in politics.

Eunice leaped in to affirm that family was important to her dear Frank, who owned half of Queensland. Even if dear Frank owned only a small sliver of Queensland it was still of great interest to my father because when he was not dreaming about being an MP he was in land and property development. It was clear that the prospect of establishing a relationship with Frank made his mouth water.

They ignored me and I was left to finish off everyone's carrot cake and watch the pigeons being outmanoeuvred by the starlings in the chase for crumbs. The pigeons were not very smart but they seemed to survive by dogged persistence. They never gave up. I was more of the pigeon mentality, I decided, I would not give up either.

'You're coming to dinner on Friday,' Eunice said to me. 'Make sure your mother doesn't come dressed like a bag lady. Tell her to come early so that I can inspect her.'

'She doesn't like the idea of pretending she's still married. Maybe it's not good for her mental health.'

'Nah,' said Eunice and my father in unison.

We put Eunice in a taxi and my father, with an 'I suppose I'd better ask' expression on his face, said 'What do you want to do, Jane?'

I let him off the hook. When I was younger I would have said, 'I want to go to Harrods to get a sundae,' or, 'Take me round the Trocadero,' but it was no fun blackmailing an ice-cream out of someone who was always looking at his watch.

I said, 'I need to get over to Vincent's. I promised to help out.'

My father looked alarmed. 'Don't get caught up in all that. Suffering and poverty are a mindset. Your mother likes suffering.'

'She doesn't have enough money to pay the rent.'

My father sighed. 'That old argument.' He looked at his

73

watch for the umpteenth time. 'Look I've got to go. Can you get yourself back on the tube?'

'Oh sure.'

'Don't sit next to a dirty old man.'

'You're the only dirty old man I know.'

He looked really perturbed by that remark.

'It's just a joke, Daddy, lighten up. By the way, could I interview you for my school project?'

'No.'

He ran down the steps to the Piccadilly underground, bought me a ticket, slipped three ten-pound notes into my hand and pushed me through the barrier. Then he ran off, looking at his watch again.

SEX 2000 – CONSUMER REPORT

Is sex your friend?

I tried out the question on Sophia first. 'Is sex your friend?' I asked her.

'What do you mean by that?'

'Well Dolores told me that sex made her believe that Vincent was attractive. Well under normal conditions anybody would need a heavy dose of a mind-altering drug to make them think that Vincent was even acceptable.'

'So what?'

'It means that a sex attack can make you imagine anything.'

'Only if you want it to,' said Sophia dismissively.

'I don't know if Dolores wanted it to. I think a sex attack is scary. It hits you like scarlet fever. You never know when you're going to feel all hot about somebody. It just comes over you like a sudden curse. And then you could end up in an alley in Shepherd's Bush for the rest of your life.'

'The thing to do,' said Sophia thoughtfully, 'is never to go into a room where you might meet somebody from an alley in Shepherd's Bush. You have to be very careful before you enter a room.'

'How awful. You can't go anywhere without worrying about it. It's like spending your life in jail.'

'Not your entire life. Once you've chosen somebody, you're safe.'

'No you're not. You might be married to a cabinet minister and go into McDonald's, get hit by the sex attack, and run off with somebody who sells you a milkshake. And then you get written about in all the tabloids.'

'But you won't be in danger for the rest of your life. By the time you get to thirty it all dies down. You get neutered and you can relax.'

'Oh God. I can't wait till I'm thirty.'

'It could be thirty-five,' said Sophia cautiously.

Conclusion: You cannot assume that sex is your friend. It can give you bad advice. To avoid making perilous sexual choices it is important to think very carefully before you go anywhere.

CHAPTER
12

Sunday morning was silent, fresh and cold; cars were parked nose to tail with frosted windows. Cats with temporary freedom of the city sauntered extravagantly down the middle of the street and, apart from the odd crisp bag flapping in the gutter, produced the only movement.

Freddy sent me out to buy some milk and coffee beans from the corner shop and sat on the sofa in his towelling dressing-gown, hair dishevelled, dark stubble on his chin, his face a death mask, as he waited for his life infusion of caffeine. When I returned, panting from running in the sharp, cold air, he spoke like a ventriloquist without moving his lips.

'Grind the beans, not too long, not too short. Get the filter, put the paper in, tip the ground coffee in and boil the water.'

I did all that while he went on sitting in his trance.

'Pour the water slowly over the coffee. Not too much water for God's sake, don't drown it.'

'What sort of mug do you want?' I asked cheerfully, looking at our collection of cracked china.

'Any damn mug will do. Pour out the coffee, put a splatter of milk in it, don't ruin it, then bring it over here and clear off.'

I brought him the coffee and watched him take the first sip like a dying man drinking the elixir of life. I folded my arms and watched him.

'You know coffee tastes like poison, it is a poison, everyone thinks it's poisonous when they have their first sip,' I informed him.

'Didn't I tell you to clear off?' He was cradling the mug in his hands, staring into the dark liquid with expressionless eyes. His white shins, like whalebones, adorned with profuse amounts of dark hair, jutted out from under his beige dressing-gown.

'I'm just trying to point out to you that if you hadn't forced yourself to like it in the first place, you wouldn't be addicted now.'

'Clear off.'

'Adults are really stupid. They do all these things they don't like at first, just so they can get addicted.'

'Clear off.'

'Do you want some more?'

'Yes.'

I brought the coffee-pot over and filled his mug to the top (the only uncracked one, decorated with the red nasturtiums).

'Now clear off,' he said.

'Freddy, what do you think of my father?'

'I think he's a wanker.'

'Do you think he could get elected as an MP?'

'Only if he became a mass hypnotist.'

'I think he could possibly pull it off. He's very good at getting his own way. I mean, you've never met him, you only know what we've told you about him.'

'I thought I told you to clear off.' He sank his chin into his chest, so that only the top of his head with its thick sprouting of dark blackberry hair was visible.

My mother and I were always trying to get advice out of Freddy because he had made the mistake of offering a few opinions about the mess we were in when he first came to live with us. My mother liked to be talked through every-thing. Freddy called it being given permission to get out of bed in the morning. And I was constantly asking him about different 'friends' at school, demanding character analysis, and an in-depth explanation as to why they didn't like me. We had devoured his advice-giving potential until it had dwindled considerably, but it occasionally resurged and gushed as new, so we were ever hopeful.

'But Freddy, what shall we do about my father? He's ganging up with Grandma Eunice now. They're going to make Louise go to dinner on Friday and pretend she's still married to him.'

I called her Louise because Freddy had once said I was going to look pretty silly calling her Mummy when I was forty, so I should wean myself of the habit early.

'How many times do I have to tell you to clear off?'

'But can't you speak to her?'

Freddy took a brief moment to look up from the swirling brown depths of his coffee. 'I can't do anything with your mother. She thinks she's a dog's turd.'

I gave up and took a mug, a small, cracked one with hunting scenes, to my mother's room where she was under the bedcovers.

'I've brought you some of Freddy's coffee,' I said, picking my way carefully over the stacked furniture.

'I heard all that.' Her voice came muffled from the depths of the bed. 'He said I'm a dog's turd.'

'No he didn't. He said you think you're a dog's turd,' I tried to explain.

'I said she *thinks* she's a dog's turd, for God's sake,' shouted Freddy from the living-room.

'Aaagh,' wailed my mother.

I tried to find a clear surface to put the coffee on, and selected an old wooden trunk with dull brass handles and corners, which was balanced on top of an Ikea chest of drawers near my mother's side of the bed. On the trunk were assorted books, papers, and socks waiting to be darned. And on top of the socks was a business card.

'What's this?' I asked, making a clearing for the coffee mug.

My mother's haunted white face emerged guiltily from under the duvet, a fat feather-duvet inherited from her richer, married days.

'Dr Jefferies gave it to me,' she mumbled cautiously.

I leaned over and looked into her face. 'Dr Jefferies? Why haven't you told me? When did he give it to you?'

'Yesterday.'

'Yesterday! I was there yesterday. You didn't say anything. What time did he come in?'

'I don't know. Maybe when you were having tea with Richard. I don't have to tell you everything. He came in because his gold stripe had finally arrived so he brought his car in and Vincent put it on. It's really boring. Do I have to tell you about every customer who comes in?'

My mother, with eyes swollen from sleep and with pillow creases like bird claws etched on her cheeks, took the coffee-mug, sipped and grimaced, then returned it to the clearing among the socks. She didn't like Freddy's strong stuff, and much preferred Twining's Assam tea but we didn't have any. Frequently we had to put up with what Freddy liked because we were in no position to complain.

I turned the card over, looking for clues. It was a plain card, with nothing but Dr Jefferies' name, address and phone number on, plus a phone number and extension at London University.

'Did he say anything?' I asked suspiciously.

'No ... well, he said to phone him if I wanted some help or something like that.' My mother tried to swallow the words so that they were not too audible.

'Some help? What kind of help?'

'He didn't say.'

I ran into the living-room holding the card high in the air. 'Did you hear that Freddy! Dr Arnold Jefferies who wrote *The Killer Instinct and You* came round to Vincent's yesterday and gave her this card. And he told her to phone him!'

Freddy didn't look up.

'I bet he wants to give her the killer instinct!' I whooped.

'If he gives it to her,' mumbled Freddy, 'she'll lose it.'

'But don't you think it's incredible? He's been on *Pebble Mill* and LBC Radio and he's told her to phone him!'

Freddy didn't reply.

I ran back into the bedroom waving the card. 'Yahoo! You'll have to phone him right now.'

'I can't.' My mother disappeared under the duvet.

'Yes you can.'

'I can't.'

'You have to phone him.'

'Why?'

'Because I want you to.'

'Why?'

'Because he might be able to help you.'

'He can't help me.'

I picked up a corner of the duvet and bellowed underneath it, 'PLEASE, please phone him. You don't know, it could be the answer.'

'I can't.'

'I don't care. You've got to.'

'I can't.'

'You've got to. You've got to do it for me!' By now I had moved up to a high-decibel whine, a sort of screeching, and my mother came out from under the duvet.

'For you?'

I was surprising myself with my degree of anger, because it was now beyond my control. I was angry with my mother for making me worry about her for my entire life. Why should she dominate my thinking so much? I was at the age when you were supposed to ignore mothers. But how could I ignore her when she was so helpless all the time?

'I can't stand it any more, watching you be so awful. I'm ashamed of you. I can't stand it. I don't want to live with you like this. You're not worth living with. You're letting me down. It's mental cruelty. You're not a proper mother. I'm cursed to have a mother like you.'

I had worked myself into quite a lather and I was crying and my voice was shaking.

My mother looked blank at first, her mouth hung slightly open, then the hurt slowly registered; her eyes began to fill with tears and her lips trembled.

'Jane – it's not true.'

'It is. It is true.'

Her lips went on trembling as she said, 'When you love somebody, you don't think they're a curse.'

'Yes you do. Because I do. You're ruining my life.'

'I don't ruin it on purpose.' Her lower lip was quivering to such an extent that the words hardly made sense.

'Yes you do. Yes you do. Because now you have a chance to get better and you won't do anything about it.'

'Jane,' she pleaded, kneading the duvet cover with her fingers. 'That man is not stable. He's a joke. Somebody who wants to help troubled people doesn't write a book called *The Killer Instinct and You*. It's just a joke. You don't want to make me part of some stupid American joke, do you?'

I jutted my own trembling lip out. 'You're already a joke. You're a walking joke.'

'That's not true.'

'It is. You know it is. And it's terrible for me. It's making me want to run away. It makes me want to go and live with Daddy. That's how terrible I feel.'

'Jane –'

'It's no use saying Jane. You're not worried about me. You're only worried about yourself. You're too shy to do anything, you're so sensitive you can't make a move. Everybody knows that being shy is just being selfish. You're extra shy so you must be extra selfish. I won't let you come to my school anymore, you're so worm-like, I can't stand it. I'm going to tell everybody you died!'

'Girls! Cool it!' yelled Freddy from the living-room.

'Shut up, Freddy!' I shouted back at him.

I was crying. My mother was crying. Then we both started howling. It was a mess. Freddy went off to his room, slammed the door shut and turned a Debussy CD up very loud.

When my mother stopped crying she crawled out of bed and wandered around the flat in a trance. The music kept on booming beautifully from under Freddy's door. 'La Mer', I think it was. It certainly sounded like the sea.

Then my mother sat down and stared at the wall. The bell from a nearby church began to toll. The church was in possession of two bells but only one was activated, so it sounded like a gong, a countdown for my mother who was running out of time.

I stayed in the bedroom but I could see her through the door. My hands felt weak, they hung by my side, dead and useless.

Finally she said in a tiny voice. 'All right. What's his number?'

I raced out of the bedroom with Dr Jefferies' card. She took it from me with an 'Are you going to let me off the hook?'

expression in her eyes but I didn't pay any attention to it and just stared meaningfully at the card.

She also stared at the card, she gave it one last lingering look before going before the firing squad. She dialled Dr Jefferies' number.

It took him some time to answer but when he did she said, 'Hello, Dr Jefferies ... I'm Louise Hampton from Vincent's Coachworks and Launderette.'

It was obvious from her deflated expression that he had no idea who she was. She threw me an 'I told you so' look and battled on.

'You gave me your card yesterday ... At Vincent's, when you came over to get your gold stripe ... Yes, and that's when you gave me your card ... well you said if I wanted any help to phone you ... Yes I'm rather desperate ...'

Dr Jefferies spoke at some length after that, while my mother nodded into the receiver.

Finally she said, 'Yes ... Yes ... Yes that would be a good time ... A notebook. Right ... Thank you very much.'

My mother, her face a flaming pink, put the phone down.

'Well?' I demanded.

'He couldn't remember giving me the card,' she said accusingly. 'And he said I couldn't be rather desperate. He said I'm either desperate or I'm not. He's really bossy. He's just the type of person I should avoid.'

'He said he wants to see you? He told you to bring a notebook?' I asked excitedly.

'He won't remember me when I get there. I'll have to explain all over again. Oh God. Why have you done this to me?'

'Are you talking to God or me?'

She didn't answer, but rested her chin on her hand, glum and deflated.

Freddy came out of his room, hugging his dressing-gown

for protection, and headed for the kitchen with his head down. 'Don't talk to me. I'm just getting more coffee.'

'She phoned him!' I said.

'Is this good?' he asked as he placed his transparent coffee-pot on to a gas-ring and turned it up high. This was the coffee-pot that came with the instructions 'Under no circumstances warm pot over direct heat'. I had been expecting it to explode or melt for months.

'No it's not good,' said my mother gloomily. 'How could you make me do that? Oh God what have I done?'

I began to get irritable. 'Oh come on. It's not that terrible.'

'He said he's going to videotape me.' My mother went into the kitchen and confronted Freddy with this horrifying proposition. She could have been telling him he was going to pull her toenails off one by one.

Freddy rinsed his cup thoughtfully. 'He wants to get the only example of a captive human invertebrate on film for all the world to see,' he said.

My mother sighed and said nothing.

I was thinking, why didn't she say something crushing to Freddy like, 'An invertebrate is not necessarily a worm, it can also be a python'. But she wouldn't and she didn't.

There was a long silence after that while my mother sat looking miserable and Freddy poured his coffee out and retreated to his room again. I went off and did some Latin homework and left my mother cleaning the kitchen floor.

I could hear the clank of the bucket and vigorous scrubbing, and then polishing. It seemed to go on forever. The kitchen was very small and the floor was covered with worn linoleum tiles. How she could extract so much work from that small patch was a puzzle to me. She stayed there for a long time making busy noises – scrubbing, rinsing, polishing – then the bucket would splash into the sink, more water would be poured out and the cycle would start again.

I had thought I didn't know how a stressed-out rat would behave. But now I knew. A stressed-out rat, in the confines of its cage, would scurry around and perform the same action again and again.

SEX 2000 – CONSUMER REPORT

How valuable is sex in advertising?

I went round to Sophia's house in Chiswick to conduct this interview.

'How valuable is sex in advertising?' I asked her.

'Jane,' said Sophia, in that superior, critical way of hers, 'it's no good interviewing me all the time. Your report's going to be really pathetic if it's not more wide ranging.'

'I know that,' I replied irritably, 'but it's hard to find people to interview.'

'There are people all over the place. Tackle them.' She looked out of her bedroom window at the crowds of beer drinkers sitting by the river.

'I will, I will.' Oh hell, I hated Sophia. 'But now I'm here, tell me this, why do advertisers put a model in a bikini on everything they want to sell?'

'Because it makes people look and then they buy whatever it is.'

'So a woman in a bikini has power, would you say?'

Sophia thought about this and said, 'Yes, she does. Perhaps I'll be a model. I'll stop eating chocolate biscuits.'

'Do you think I could be a model?'

Sophia looked me over. 'No. Thirteen's too young to diet, you should wait till your birthday, and anyway, you'd have to give up a lot more than chocolate biscuits.'

I winced and retorted, 'You don't want to be a model, it would be a waste of your education.'

85

'Jane,' she said reprovingly, 'you could go to university for years trying to work out how to make people buy things. Or, you could put on a bikini and just get on with it.'

I felt gloomy about that. 'I suppose they're right when they say women don't need an education. All they need is a bikini.'

'Absolutely. A thong bikini.'

'I suppose if women Members of Parliament wore bikinis they'd be listened to far more in the House of Commons.'

'Oh yes,' agreed Sophia enthusiastically, 'everyone would watch it on TV. I would.'

I picked up my clipboard and pen and tried to think up an intelligent conclusion.

'Why do we look at other women in bikinis? We have our own bikinis, and anyway we see ourselves in the bath. It's not a mystery is it?'

'That's a very good point, Jane. I haven't a clue though.' Sophia was bored by then and refused to discuss it anymore.

When I got home my mother, still depressed and staring into the sink, helped me with my conclusion.

She said, 'Women stare at other women in bikinis because they've been taught to be interested in the things that interest men.'

'You mean, they have lessons?'

'No, it's much more subtle than that.'

'So how do they get taught?'

My mother stared deeply into the sink-hole for the answer to that. 'It's what goes on inside men's minds. They have the power so they get to have a ... what's the word ... they get to have a monopoly on all the fantasies in the world, so then we have their fantasies and dream their dreams.'

'Are you sure that's right? I don't want Mrs Cassels yelling at me for getting it wrong.'

Without taking her eyes off the sink-hole, my mother answered, 'I think it's right. I've given these things a lot of thought. Thinking is what I'm good at.' Then she looked up and said meaningfully, 'It's a compensation.'

'Well Mrs Cassels is always nagging about accuracy in consumer reporting. She says we can't fiddle the statistics.'

'Ask somebody else then.'

'No. This'll do.'

Conclusion: Sex is useful in advertising. It is extremely fortunate for advertisers that women have always been very obedient. If men think something's exciting, women think it's exciting too. A female in a thong bikini can attract the attention of both men and women. Therefore advertisers kill two birds with one stone and save themselves a lot of money.

CHAPTER
13

My mother insisted that I went with her to Dr Jefferies' house. She really *insisted* and it occurred to me that she was extremely tough about insisting how weak she was and how much she needed someone to prop her up. I picked up an abandoned baby bird once, it was almost featherless and its little wings were useless twigs, but once in my hand its tiny claw-feet pushed forcefully on my palms. There was so much life in those claws that I've wondered ever since if power and life weren't the same thing; that we all have power because we're alive but we use it in different ways, and that my mother was using it to be weak. She would have told me I was dead wrong but I often thought that was the case.

We went to Dr Jefferies' before work. It was not yet seven o'clock in the morning, snail-trails of frost were on the car window, and the side streets were still asleep. And so was I. I have always needed to lie in bed for ten minutes to find out who I am. Instead I had to scoop up all my schoolbooks in frantic shovelfuls and pull on the first thing I could find. Perhaps I had stepped into a pillow case, I couldn't tell.

I was really annoyed with my mother for dragging me out. Why couldn't she be motherly and supportive instead of being so zealously weak?

I had discovered that the world was divided into those

who found girls of thirteen a source of considerable inquiry
and those who found them of absolute no interest whatsoever. Dr Jefferies belonged to the latter group. When I
walked into his front hall he looked at me as if I were
causing a particularly bad smell. Admittedly I had not
washed. I was not much of a washer in those days but I
didn't think I was that bad.

'What's she doing here?' he asked. His hair was completely flat on one side, where he must have slept on it, while
the other side stuck out at a sort of right angle.

My mother opened her mouth to explain but nothing
came out.

So I said, 'She needs moral support.'

'Moral support,' he repeated as if that were an obscene
concept to him and then grunted something about following
him.

He went up the stairs, past his study with its three desks,
and floor piled high with a snowstorm of assorted papers
and books, along the landing to a large room that would
have swallowed our entire flat in one mouthful.

The room had perfect floorboards, that is to say, they were
not cracked or worn like the front door and were discreetly
burnished. The floorboards were the outstanding feature of
the room as it was otherwise entirely empty apart from a
desk and two wooden chairs at one end. With some long,
gilt mirrors the room would have made a perfect dance
studio. There were high, open windows with floating net
curtains rustling in the breeze, like ballet girls' skirts, at
either end of the room. The window at one end looked out
over the street and our sturdy Hillman Imp, which was
parked under a fancy Royal Borough of Kensington and
Chelsea Edwardian-style streetlamp; the window at the
other end looked over a wild garden, full of vines that had
been let loose to wander this way and that, meet others and

intertwine. There were sprouting flagstones, rich with feathery weeds, a pond, a mossy stone cherub and bushes lathering out of old tubs unfettered by any pruning. Beyond this secret garden were the much tidier communal gardens with their clipped pathways, and a forest of trees, sycamore, oak, willow and pine. I could have sat by that window forever.

We followed Dr Jefferies to the end of the long, empty room to the lone desk at the end. As we drew closer we noticed a tabby cat with a torn ear asleep on one of the chairs. Dr Jefferies sat on the other chair and I slid down the wall and sat on the floor, leaving the cat for my mother. She stood over the chair looking apologetically at the cat. She was observed by Dr Jefferies.

'The cat responds only to kicking,' he told her. 'You will be required to kick the cat every morning.'

My mother looked even more apologetically at the cat who went on sleeping.

'Yah!' yelled Dr Jefferies, and my mother almost jumped out of her skin. She couldn't take any kind of sudden noise. If a balloon burst she would always have a mini nervous breakdown. The cat opened one eye, got up, stretched lazily and jumped off the chair and my mother sat down quickly before it changed its mind.

Dr Jefferies leaned back and put his hands behind his head, showing a hole under one arm of his blue shirt. 'Up front, we'll discuss fees. It's obvious you can't pay me, so I'm not even going to ask. All I ask of you is that you allow me to write about you in my next book as a case study. I won't use your real name. And no one here will read it anyway. I write mainly for the American market. The British aren't interested in a good, clean killer instinct. They're not straight like the Americans. They like to cut your throat politely and have you smile and thank them while they're doing it.'

My mother threw a glance at me. Did she expect me to protest on her behalf? I couldn't tell. I didn't see anything so terrible in being a case study: not when you had as many problems as my mother.

A beam of wintry sunlight fell on the desk in front of Dr Jefferies as he took a pen from his breast pocket and pulled a notebook out of a drawer.

'Have you always been ineffectual?' he asked.

My mother looked worried as if it were a trick question but she eventually answered, 'As far as I can remember.'

'You like to please don't you?'

'Yes.'

'Yes,' he sighed, 'you would say yes. The first thing you will have to realise is that it's a trap. You must give up trying to please. I'm going to drill that into your head. It will get there by a process of attrition. Say to yourself, I will give up trying to please. Let me hear you say that.'

My mother spoke in a barely audible whisper. 'I will give up trying to please.'

A distant raking in the garden below was far noisier than my mother's timorous voice but it seemed to satisfy Dr Jefferies.

'Good,' he said. 'Because it's a complete waste of time. For one thing people don't know what they want. So you'll never please them. And on top of that you're eroding yourself until people feel they're not relating to anything. And in your case you've become totally invisible.'

'Yes,' whispered my mother.

'Every single effort of yours to be liked, to please, will be rewarded with self-hate and hidden rage.'

'Oh.'

'Oh yes,' he said, flipping his pen over, 'and what we have to do is to bring out that rage, turn it away from yourself and project it outwards.'

91

'Oh.'

'What we want here is an explosion of rage, of massive energy pouring forth. You are going to amaze and frighten people.'

'Oh,' repeated my mother, gazing at me with an expression of total disbelief on her face.

The expression transferred itself to Dr Jefferies' face. He began jutting his chin forward in the way I had noticed him do before, tapping his top front teeth against his bottom teeth.

'It's hard to know where to begin,' he mused.

The tabby cat returned to sit in the doorway, waiting for us to give up on the impossible project and give him back his chair in the sun.

Dr Jefferies threw his pen on to the desk. 'I'm going to have to ask you a lot of questions about yourself. But I think before we can even start on that we need something simple, just to get you out of the mud.' He sighed pessimistically and ran his fingers through his thick, tufty hair. 'What we're going to start with is pure physical aggression.'

My mother, a progressively forlorn, sagging creature, sat hunched on the hard wooden chair, hugging herself protectively. Dr Jefferies studied this pathetic specimen.

'Throw out your chest,' he ordered, 'or whatever you call it. Your chest will have to see the light of day if we're going to get anywhere. I'm going to send you to some karate classes. I want you to learn some self-defence. Go on some assault courses. Overcome physical fear. We need to bring out a physical expression of what you're going to do mentally. I want you to run. You're going to go in training like an athlete.'

'Could I go to the—?' asked my mother, already halfway out of her chair. She headed for the door with the speed of light. We could hear her running down the stairs and Mrs

Moon coming out of the kitchen and making solicitous noises.

Dr Jefferies looked over at me, slumped quietly against the wall, sniffing the agreeable smell of the polished floor.

He sighed and asked, 'Is she always like this?'

'Not always.'

Dr Jefferies sighed again, picked up his pen and started tapping it on the desk. 'I don't know. I don't know. I can't promise anything.'

He couldn't promise anything! This from the man who made wild promises on the radio and television about how he could give any man or mouse the killer instinct.

As if reading my mind he said, 'I can't turn her around if she doesn't co-operate. If she's going to be running out of the room all the time it's impossible.'

'I'll talk to her,' I said, trying to sound confident.

He was not listening. He stared at his watch, indicating that he'd moved on. Then he sniffed and I was gone. As far as he was concerned I was no longer in that room. The cat had far more claim to existence than I had. Feeling this, the cat strutted importantly across the floor and reclaimed my mother's chair, puts its front paws together neatly, like a knife and fork on a plate, close and tidy, at the end of the meal. The cat had signed my mother's expulsion order, the end of her killer instinct lessons. She had proved to be unpromising material.

What could I do? What cards did I have up my sleeve? I knew I could not beg Dr Jefferies for a second chance or burst into tears and appeal to his niceness, warmth, or milk of human kindness. He did not seem to have any.

Oh hell. I was tired of worrying about my mother. I wanted to give up all that worrying about her and devote it all to myself. Girls of my age worried about themselves all the time, it was their vocation, whereas I could only worry about myself as a very small hobby. I was deprived.

The cat yawned and made itself comfortable. It was preparing itself for a nice long nap. Dr Jefferies looked at his watch again and gave me a long piercing look. 'You seem to have very little of your mother's reticence,' he said, rather accusingly.

In those days I was a little hazy about the meaning of reticence but I wasn't going to admit it.

'I would like to have much more reticence,' I replied, 'but she's got it all. I mean, she took my share. I'm hoping that after she's studied with you we can share it out. You know, so it's more balanced.'

I was extremely pleased with myself for getting the conversation around to the subject of my mother's future lessons.

It seemed to remind Dr Jefferies of why we were there. He went downstairs and found my mother skulking in the kitchen with Mrs Moon. He turned Mrs Moon out of the kitchen by shouting, 'Get out Mrs Moon!' and continued the class there among the saucepans and cups and saucers for another half an hour. He spent a lot of the time criticising my mother for being British. He said the British had two religions: the class system and the welfare state, and they were both imploding like black holes, whatever that meant.

My mother promised that she would return the next morning, and continue every day until, in the words of Dr Jefferies, 'we've licked this thing'. It was a good beginning after all.

Then we all dispersed. My mother went to work, Dr Jefferies went off to give a lecture, and I went to school where I discovered that I was wearing my mother's awful black, misshapen cardigan and one of her skirts, a sensible blue cotton skirt that had middle-aged respectability written all over it. I had dragged them on in a hurry when I fell out of bed. Where was the street cred, the threat, the tough urban look? There was hardly one girl in my class who did not come over to ask, 'Why are you wearing *that*?'

SEX 2000 – CONSUMER REPORT

How hygienic is sex?

During break Sophia told me that she had been to a party at Annabel's house. How she got herself invited I don't know, although I suspected that she'd gatecrashed because nobody invited Sophia, or me for that matter, to anything.

Annabel was in the year above us and therefore, like all of her ilk, had slightly more advanced occasions than the girls in our year. The gory details of these parties filtered down to the girls in my year who were anxious to learn the form. The parties seemed to have fixed ingredients. Boys who arrived with alcohol and spliffs hidden under their jackets. Much drunken staggering about. A Vesuvius of puffing on tobacco and marijuana. And as much 'getting off' as the partygoer could fit in.

'Do you know that girl who played the duke in *Twelfth Night*?' asked Sophia who was sitting on a wall eating a Crunchie.

'Yes,' I said.

'Well she gave someone a blow job.'

I had only recently learned this term but tried to appear nonchalant.

'A boy?' I asked.

'Who else, you daft knob.'

'How do you know?'

'It was general knowledge. Everyone was walking in and out, hither and yon. Hard to avoid really.'

'Why did she do it? It couldn't be any fun for her.'

'She was being a good sport I suppose.'

'What did she do with the stuff that came out?' I asked. 'Did she swallow it?'

'I don't know,' Sophia admitted.

'What does it look like?'

'If my information is correct it's like an egg-white with a little snot thrown in.'

'Ugh! Sophia, don't be disgusting!'

'Did you know that waiters squirt it into the soup of bad-tempered customers?'

'Ugh! I'll never have soup again.'

'Anyway it was a fine party. You would have loved it.'

'It sounds like an orgy,' I remarked.

Sophia paused mid-munch of her chocolate bar to look pityingly critical of my over-reaction. 'It was just your common, garden variety party, Jane. Don't get your knickers in a twist.'

'Well would your mother let you have that kind of party?'

'I'd make quite sure she went out. Annabel's mother was a little hysterical when she came back, of course, but that was because of the smoke mostly. Everyone had been at it like chimneys and a lot of them haven't a clue about ashtrays so the carpet looked rather gritty.'

I was still mesmerised by the news about the blow job.

'Do you think everybody does it?' I asked Sophia.

'It's pretty compulsory. I mean if you want to be a real nerd you don't have to do it before you get married but you do after. Because then everyone's worried about getting bored.'

I was really disappointed that people did that sort of thing. In fact the whole idea made me puke. I couldn't believe that adults who were always telling me to wash apples before eating them were the same ones who were doing this extremely unhygienic thing. By the time they had done it, surely, they were covered with germs.

Sophia finished her Crunchie and jumped down from the wall.

'Must dash. Gotta cram in some geography before the test.'

Conclusion: Sex is pretty worrying for beginners who are concerned about hygiene and some tasks can seem gruesome. However, other beginners have less concern and find it easier to reach the required standard.

CHAPTER

14

'Cyrus has left me in debt,' Grandma Eunice told my mother. 'My last chance is this dinner.'

'But . . .' said my mother.

'Louise! This is life and death! If you and Richard don't come and help me out I may end up in a cardboard box under Waterloo Bridge.'

'But . . .'

'It's the smallest thing. All you have to do is dress nicely, look acceptable to Frank, and act positive.'

'But Richard and I—'

'Louise! I'm so close now, it won't take much. Frank is a lonely man. He wants a warm, loving family. He actually told me that, I'm not making this up. He misses it and we can provide him with it.'

'Warm and loving?'

'With style. If you have nothing to wear, I'll send you something over. For God's sake, Louise, don't embarrass me. Don't say a word about being a washerwoman.'

Eunice's bag of clothes, sent in a taxi, raised far more problems than it solved. So my mother and I made an assault on Freddy's room, charging through the barriers of tripods, lighting equipment and black plastic, and dragging out some of his jackets and silk shirts; he was not appreciative. 'How come I'm the only one you rob, cheat and steal from? You eat my food, wear my clothes, give me all the bills. What am I? Your release valve? Contrary to popular belief, I'm not a millionaire. The reason I'm living in this shack is because I've fallen on hard times. Look at me, working all hours, trying to make enough to get out of here.'

He was sitting cross-legged on his bed with a set of photographs on his lap, retouching each one, nimbly removing a wrinkle here a spot there, and with the finest of razors scratching away bags from under the eyes.

'Don't go to dinner with the old grandma,' he said, 'unless she pays you. It's a PR job you're doing. Get her to pay you well. Then you can stop ripping me off.'

He carefully smoothed away a double chin from a ten-by-eight matt-finish. 'Charge her a fee. You're helping to launch a product on to the market – a second-hand, worn product. It's going to require heavy promotion. That's expensive. And if you wear my Armani jacket I'm billing her for the rental.'

He thought about it some more as we threw garments left and right. 'You're perpetrating a fraud. I mean, let's face it. It's a con trick. If you're dragged into a con trick of this dimension and she pulls it off, then she should pay you half the proceeds.'

'What could that be?' I asked, as I tried one of his dark-blue shirts over my jeans.

'You can't wear jeans,' my mother said.

'Well, this poor old unsuspecting guy you're setting up owns half of Queensland,' said Freddy.

'I think he only owns a small part of Queensland.'

'It sounds good to me. Take a percentage.'

My mother gave up trying to look sophisticated in Freddy's jacket and returned to the familiarity of her cardigan collection and the bag of clothes Eunice had sent over. It contained, among other things, a navy-blue cash-mere blazer with large, ornate gold buttons. It matched nothing.

'Navy blue is notoriously difficult to match,' my mother said.

'It is if you don't have anything. You need a white blouse and skirt, and navy blue shoes,' I told her, knowing full well she had nothing of the kind in her small Gothic brown and black collection.

Eunice had also sent over two gold lamé blouses, but nothing to go with them, and a large black crêpe cocktail dress with tassels that sagged obscenely at the chest revealing vast expanses of frayed underwear, and a pink linen suit that my mother had no shoes for. She owned one pair of black shoes with heels; the rest of her shoes were worn trainers and walking boots.

After hours of opening drawers and cupboards hoping for the perfect solution to jump out, my mother ended up wearing the old brown Laura Ashley dress, the one she had worn to Grandpa Cyrus' funeral, with the navy-blue blazer. They looked horrendous together, but we decided that the jacket was cashmere and the buttons were so ostentatious and expensive looking that they would have the required effect, which was of course, to look wealthy. She wore them with some huge gilt earrings and bracelet of Eunice's which also added to the desired flashiness.

I was a problem. I wanted to hang on to my jeans. But my mother was prepared to stage a mini breakdown if I did, so she won. I eventually chose the black cocktail dress, which I pinned at the back to prevent the sagging, and wore Freddy's black Armani jacket over it to hide safety pins and bulges. I actually thought I looked quite striking, although my mother would have preferred it if I'd chosen a 'more youthful' colour.

We went to Freddy for inspection before we set out.

'You look like a couple of Brazilian pygmies who've unpacked their first Oxfam hamper.'

'No, really,' insisted my mother.

'You look like a rich tart,' he said.

'How about me?' I asked.

'You look like a trainee tart.'

Grandma Eunice lived in a small, mock-Georgian house in a purged, spruce street, where she could see into Holland Park itself if she leaned out of her bedroom window: 'a real selling point', she frequently pointed out. My mother and I walked there as it was only a mile or so away from the less fragrant realities of our flat.

En route we passed the house where a swimming pool had been put under the driveway. Over the previous months we had watched as huge diggers and cranes had removed tons of earth, driven massive iron pilings into the deep and then poured in tons of concrete. We were there the day the jacuzzi was swung into place and we goggled in consternation. How could they fit that monster in? We had taken such an interest we felt it was our pool, but now it had all disappeared under the driveway and was out of our reach. Somewhere down there, in the depths of the earth, walled by the dark worm-filled soil, millions of years old, was the pool, steaming in its tiled container pod and smart mosaics, etherealised by subtle lighting, no longer our pool.

According to plan we met my father, who was waiting in his BMW, in the shadows near Grandma Eunice's house. My mother and he slipped on large gold wedding rings that Eunice had provided for the occasion.

'It's like being in a movie,' I said.

My father grasped my shoulders and dug his nice clean fingernails into the bony part of my shoulders, one of my rare bony parts. 'Jane. Co-operate. No sarky comments. I want you to be the model of a perfect English schoolgirl. We're a team. Everyone has to play his part or we'll go under.'

He meant that he would not be able to make any real-estate deals with Frank if we didn't snare him into the family.

'We're in a recession,' my father warned me, 'we don't let opportunities like this slip through our fingers. Life's been too easy for you. You don't know what it is to struggle for something.'

'What am I getting out of it?' I asked.

'Don't be daft,' he snapped.

'And what's she getting out of it?' I indicated my mother who was fiddling with her wedding ring as if it were a tight handcuff; all rings gave her claustrophobia.

My father gaped at my mother with his mouth at half-mast as he tried to come up with a creative answer.

'The satisfaction of a job well done,' he said finally. 'And remember this isn't a dress rehearsal, this is the real thing.'

We walked past a row of mock-Georgian clones of Eunice's house. The well-lit interiors displayed almost identical chandeliers, lamps, vases and sensible works of art in each house. And we, three happy family clones, stepped obediently on to Eunice's doorstep.

Grandma Eunice, wearing the ultimate power-dressing ensemble, understated, carefully coutured grey silk with just enough diamonds, did not like my mother's country-style dress with the very urban cashmere jacket. Her mouth went very tight when she opened the door and squinted into the half-light.

Thinking that Frank was within earshot she said, 'What a surprising combination, Louise. Only you could think that up!'

And then when she realised that Frank had wandered out

to the back garden, she asked in a hoarse stage whisper, 'What do you mean by wearing that sack cloth again? Haven't we suffered enough of it already?'

'It's Laura Ashley.'

'Yes it's absolutely lovely for some things, it would be wonderful for hoeing. We're not hoeing this evening.'

The guest of honour wandered back from the garden accompanied by an exquisitely dressed Aunt Joanna, and we all filed into the living room to be introduced.

Frank, pink-cheeked, healthy and wholesome, his silver hair shining like a tinsel milk-bottle top, stood in front of the fireplace looking solid and rich. As we circled him we seemed like safari hunters who had sighted a particularly fine beast.

This beast, in my opinion, was far too good a catch for Eunice. He was surprisingly tuned in, so much so that I wondered why on earth he was there. Perhaps he was hypnotised by Grandma Eunice and couldn't help himself. He was obviously an international man without a discernible accent, which made me think of yachts on the Pacific. I hoped for his sake that he got away.

The evening was a success. There was never a gap in the conversation because my father could always be relied upon to waffle on about politics and Eunice waffled on about crime in the area and the declining flavour in vegetables and fruit. Aunt Joanna talked about house prices. Frank showed a great interest. My mother nodded and agreed with everyone. And I ate.

I was known for my eating ability. As my mother had never been a good provider of food I had always taken advantage of dinners out, where I ate as much as I could to make up for lost opportunities. I was desperate to broaden my eating range from the meagre fare offered by my mother. It was not only lack of money that prevented her from putting a wider selection in our refrigerator, it was also her conviction that food was the enemy. It contained preservatives, pesticides, cholesterol. There was not one item of food that received her unreserved blessing. It was all allowed in reluctantly and with suspicion.

Eunice's dinner was a free-flowing banquet for me. There was plenty of everything, creamy sauces, heaps of hot rolls and unsalted butter, as much butter as I liked. Frank's presence meant that no one could reprimand me for being a pig and I stocked up. I even put a couple of things in the pocket of Freddy's jacket and ate them later; although I received bitter complaints about sticky crumbs getting caught in the lining. I had two helpings of Bombe Francillon, a sort of bomb-shaped pudding with a casing made of coffee ice-cream, plus several chocolate truffles provided by Frank.

As I was cleaning the last speckles of bombe from my plate Frank asked me, as people often did, 'And how's school, Jane?'

I answered, of course, 'Fine.'

But he wasn't satisfied with that. 'Studying for your GCSEs?'

'Not yet,' I said.

Then he asked, 'And do you do extra-curricular projects?'

I was not quite sure what extra-curricular meant but I said, 'Yes I do actually.'

My mother made a signal to me. She crossed her eyes by looking at the end of her nose. It was meant to signify that I was in shark-infested water. But I did not pay much attention because she was always doing that. Everything was shark-infested as far as she was concerned. In fact, for her, life was a shark.

'What kind of projects?' asked Frank kindly.

'Well,' I said, 'I'm working on a project for my sociology class.'

'And what's that?'

'Well, we're looking at the last decade of the century and doing a sort of consumer report on basic things in life—'

'How about coffee?' said Eunice. 'Shall we go to the other room?' She stood up suddenly and fluffed her grey silk around her hips.

Frank leaned over the table, looking interested. 'And what do you consider are the basic things in life?'

'Well some girls in my class are doing Travel 2000, and others are doing Fashion 2000 or Food 2000. I'm doing Sex 2000.'

'Sex 2000?'

'Yes, it was a sort of a dare really. It's really hard work because there's so much to learn.'

My father, whose nose now had a friendly, wine-soaked sheen, leaned forward to join Frank. 'Well what do you say? Shall we have some coffee?'

But Frank was persistent. 'What have you learnt so far?'

'Well Freddy said sex was life. He lives with us so it was easy for me to corner him.'

'And why do you think Freddy says sex is life?' Frank asked earnestly.

'I don't know really. He's living off letters at the moment because his boyfriend's in Winnipeg. I don't know how much sex you can get out of a letter. I'll have to do some research.'

'Jane,' Grandma Eunice said in a strangled voice, 'go and switch the coffee-pot on. It's all set up.' She flashed one dagger stare at me and then led everyone out of the dining-room.

I went to switch the coffee-pot on and pocketed a few chocolate biscuits. When I came back they were all talking about flower-beds. Then they talked about weathered terra-cotta pots and how it was the time for daffodils and

105

hyacinths, and how if you wanted ivy in your window box you needed well drained, alkaline potting mixture. They were quite intense about it all, and if I as much as opened my mouth, Eunice gave me the worst killer-look ever.

Later, when we were walking with my father to his car, still pretending that we were driving off together in our happy nuclear family, my father snarled, 'What was all that twaddle about, Jane? Do you realise you screwed up the entire evening?'

'I didn't do anything wrong,' I whined.

'I couldn't believe it when you started talking about Freddy.'

'What's wrong with that?'

'Only losers have lodgers, Jane.'

'Sorry.'

'He's going to be asking himself, Who the hell's Freddy?'

'Sorry.'

'Sorry's not good enough, Jane. There we were pretending to be a happy family, sitting on a knife edge, and then you come up with a lodger. It turned the whole thing into a farce. It made us look stupid. And the sex survey! You don't talk like that to someone of his generation, they can't handle it. He was shocked to hear a school girl talking like that. Didn't you see his face? I can't believe this kid. What the hell have you been doing with her, Louise? Aren't you giving her any guidance for God's sake? The kid is not balanced, she's getting like you.'

'I am not!' I protested hotly.

My father drove off disgruntled. And we walked back over the railway bridge, now beautifully painted, with all the workmen departed. The last boards and barriers had been removed, the fresh, unmarked paving stones glistened white and virginal in the moonlight. The council's surprising choice of a fluorescent lime stripe on each bright green panel of the bridge shone like toy soldiers. It was new born.

However on the Hammersmith side, not of course on the Kensington and Chelsea side, some wag had discovered the Port-a-loo, the last item left behind by the workmen, and they had tipped it over as a great joke. Human excrement and chemicals had spewed abundantly over the shining white pavement and blotted the new bridge's first day.

My mother and I passed by on the other side in silence.

'Don't worry,' I said. 'After a few more classes with Dr Jefferies you'll be able to say bugger off to Daddy.'

'Don't swear, Jane.'

'Bugger off isn't swearing. Everyone says bugger off.'

'No they don't.'

'Yes they do.'

SEX 2000 – CONSUMER REPORT

Question: How satisfying is sex?

I discussed this with Sophia. 'If sex brings satisfaction,' I told her, 'then the people who have the most sex should be the most satisfied.'

Sophia thought about that briefly and then concluded, 'Yes I'm sure that's right.'

'So,' I said, 'if I look around for some very satisfied people I can assume that they're having a great deal of sex.'

'Absolutely,' said Sophia.

'Who is the most satisfied person you know?'

'The most satisfied person I know, by a long shot, is Juliette.'

Juliette was Sophia's three-year-old sister.

'Can't you think of anyone else?' I asked hopefully.

'No, not really. Everyone else I know is dissatisfied for one reason or another.'

'Can you explain that?'
'No, it's inexplicable,' said Sophia.
Inexplicable. I thought that was a really good word.

Conclusion: Sex is extremely satisfying but not that satisfying. Almost everyone seems dissatisfied. Some people who do not have any sex at all seem inexplicably satisfied.

CHAPTER
15

Dr Jefferies was waiting for us in his Ford Escort outside a church hall in Notting Hill. The wind was shooting icy draughts along the street and shaking the blossom off the trees, causing it to rain down on the Escort's roof. It made me sad to see that pink and white confetti falling in such profusion. After struggling through a long grey winter, I had looked on the blossom as a touch of heaven, put there to cheer me up. But it was whisked away so quickly, it didn't seem right. Surely it was a designer fault that blossom was so insecurely fastened to the branches? It was literally showering down. Some of it fell on Dr Jefferies' head as he leaned out of his window.

'What's she doing here?' he frowned at me.

He looked at my mother but she wasn't prepared to say that she'd forced me to come with her. The awful thought came to me again as I watched these two very different people staring at each other that my mother could be Dr Jefferies' one big failure, the one who wore him down and broke his trust in his great new theory.

'She can't do the class with you,' he said waspishly.

Fine. I had no desire to learn karate, or anything that involved sweaty competition. I did not enjoy exhibiting my physical inferiority on a regular basis.

I was allowed to sit in a corner while my mother was lectured by Joe, the karate instructor, about her woefully inadequate sweatpants with the threadbare seat. Joe, a man with leathery skin and broad shoulders, placed my mother at the back of a class of about twelve students. The class was asked to take a vigorous leap forward and land in an aggressive stance and all, apart from my mother, did it superbly well. She flapped her arms like a wounded pigeon and hopped a very small distance.

Dr Jefferies took Joe on one side and had a word with him. The two men put their heads together and whispered intently, looking up from time to time to send searching glances towards my mother, who tried to disappear through a crack in the coconut matting.

After that it seemed that karate went out of the window and the class was subjected to a bout of childish exercises aimed at getting my mother to open up. This diversion must have been quite galling to serious karate students, and it certainly looked as if most of them were in deadly earnest, but Joe did not seem to mind. The others had to go along with it whether they approved or not.

Why did Joe comply so willingly? Perhaps this was another example of the killer instinct at work.

Joe told the class, 'Imagine you are protecting a small child that a dangerous animal is about to snatch up in its mouth. If you yell loud enough the animal will go away. So ...' He waved his arm and the entire class, including my mother, leaped forward and screamed. They made a tremendous racket.

Then each student had to come forward one by one and save the imaginary child. There were some impressive demonstrations of lung power until my mother came forward and produced a tiny squawk, which sounded like a disgruntled chicken.

110

'No,' said Joe. 'I'm afraid the animal got the child. Try again. Only you can save this poor helpless child who has no mother. And . . .'

My mother jumped, waved her arms and squawked more loudly, sounding this time more like an irritated peahen.

She was made to repeat the exercise over and over. Eventually she made quite a creditable noise; it was nothing that would scare a wild, ferocious beast, but it was enough to put a small look of relief on Dr Jefferies' face.

'I see possibilities,' he told my mother. 'At least we know you're alive. That's a start.'

When the class was over and we were walking through the shadowy street to our cars, treading on the carpet of fallen blossom, Dr Jefferies said, 'That was a good start.'

'Oh, no, not really,' said my mother.

Dr Jefferies snapped, 'I said it was good didn't I? Accept it for God's sake.'

His thick sprouty hair seemed to get more wired up with his anger, even his eyebrows seemed to be bristling with a little added electricity. He was not a bad-looking man for someone of that fortyish age group but there was not an ounce of comfort in him.

My mother always smiled and looked helpless when she made anyone angry, but Dr Jefferies was staring at her so hard that the smile froze behind her eyes before it made it to her face.

'I hate that modest British crap,' he went on. 'The British are dishonest and compulsively modest. In their twisted minds modesty is somehow good. They like it because it's bloodless. The British don't like anything with too much life in it. They stick pokers up their asses to keep life out. The most admired British are dead, you know why?'

'No,' said my mother.

'Because a corpse is really modest. You're going to have

111

to drop a few national characteristics. You're pathologically modest, self-effacing. Have you any idea why that is?'

'Because I'm British?' she asked tentatively.

'Because you are, as we say in the trade, seeking glory through martyrdom.'

'Oh,' said my mother.

On the way home in the car my mother said, 'I wish I hadn't got involved in this.'

'You're in it now,' I said. 'You can't get out.'

My mother sighed the deepest of sighs, right from the depth of her timid soul. And then she sighed again.

We left one bad-tempered male only to meet another in the shape of my father who was sitting in our flat waiting for us to get back. It was a rare visit indeed. The last time he had been near our flat was four years previously and that was a flying visit to pick up his collection of long-playing records, an uncategorizable collection with torn covers, of such artists as the Mamas and Papas, Leonard Cohen, Chico Hamilton, and Stanley Black and his Orchestra playing 'Festival In Costa Rica'. I knew them well because we had very little else.

'Where the hell have you been?' my father asked irritably, picking bits of feather from his suit. The sofa shed feathers on all who sat on it, which according to my mother was a sign of quality.

My mother looked blank. 'Where have I been?'

At that moment Freddy came out of his room and went into the bathroom with a dripping wet film held high in the air.

'And who the hell's he?' asked my father.

'That's Freddy,' I said.

'The lodger?'

'He's paying rent and feeding us,' I said enthusiastically.

'The food was terrible before he came. Mostly baked beans, now we have avocados and garlic sausage and croissants, everything, things have really improved.'

My father gave a disparaging grunt.

'He's here because we need him,' my mother said with a hint of criticism.

'You wouldn't need him if you managed your life better,' said my father. 'I'm going up before a selection committee on Monday. I'm telling them we're still together.'

'What about Debbie?' I asked.

Debbie had done some temporary work at my father's office and had been living in his flat for the past six months.

'Debbie will have to go,' said my father. "She's absolutely useless. I considered her as a possibility and I told her she'd have to stop wearing all that stuff she gets herself up in if she's going to look right but she refuses. She says it's a point of honour. So I told her she'd have to go.'

'What stuff does she get herself up in?' I asked curiously. 'She always looks all right to me.'

'She would look all right to you,' said my father dismissively. 'They're going to ask me about my marriage. And I thought, what the hell, I have a wife and daughter already. Louise, you'd look respectable in a good suit. Eunice says she'll take you to Dickens and Jones.'

My mother and I were both thinking roughly the same thing. What about love? Hadn't he loved Debbie? Or even liked her? Was she leaving without putting up a fight?

My father anticipated an argument by saying, 'You can never divorce once you've had a child. Jane has cemented us together. Once a parent, always a parent.'

'There's something wrong here,' said my mother as she collapsed wearily into a chair. 'We divorced because we couldn't live together. We'll still have the same problems.'

'That's the beauty of the whole thing,' said Richard

113

triumphantly. 'If I get selected and then, God willing, get elected, we don't have to live together. We only have to get together for functions. All you'll need is a good wardrobe and Eunice will see to that. And the hair,' he added quickly, 'you'll have to go the hairdresser's once a week. Hair is important.'

'We'd get found out,' said my mother.

'Found out? How could we get found out? Come on, Louise, play ball. I need every bit of help I can get. And a wife and a child are an asset. I'd be a fool to waste them.' My father leaned back on the sofa and collected another coating of feathers on his navy blue suit.

'You'd have to get me some clothes too, I don't have a thing to wear,' I said.

My father gave me a hard, piercing stare. 'I'm going to keep you out of the way as much as possible. You'll be a photo opportunity. You smile and then go right back in your cage. Don't start talking about sex surveys or lodgers.'

'Could I go to French Connection and Miss Selfridge? All you have to do is give me the money and I'll go shopping myself. I don't need Grandma Eunice.'

'Oh sure,' huffed my father, 'I'm going to hand you a bunch of money and let you run all over London. You need supervision my girl, you've been let loose too long. When your father's a Member of Parliament you'll have to tow the line.'

My mother was quietly groaning with exhaustion in the background. The long day in the launderette and the leaping about in the karate class were beginning to get to her.

'Isn't it a bit early to count on that?' she asked weakly. 'Are you sure you'll get selected.'

Richard looked disappointed. 'Hark at the voice of doubt! Where's your faith in me? The road's hard but it helps if I get a little backing from my family.'

My mother's mouth fell open a little in an attempt to frame a reply. What could she say to this virtual stranger who was now staking a claim on family loyalty? Being my mother, she said nothing.

'Things will be better when you have the killer instinct,' I whispered in her ear.

She did not respond but simply sat there, floppy as a rag doll, with her eyes half rolling up every few seconds showing white eyeballs. This was a very nasty habit of hers when she became overly tired. It made her look like a ghoul.

'I've got to go,' said my father, standing up and revealing a sizeable coating of feathers on his rear. 'I don't like parking my car in this neighbourhood. You better come to me next time. We'll have to discuss strategy.'

After he'd gone my mother said, 'I wish he'd make up his mind. Either I'm a mental case or I'm a potential MP's wife.'

'I think it's great. We'll be able to get some clothes out of it. Lots of clothes. We can't be photographed by the press wearing the same outfit twice.'

My mother yawned miserably. 'Photographed by the press. What press? If you were a selection committee would you select Richard? For a start he knows absolutely nothing about politics. It's another of his whims. I was one of his whims, I should know. He liked me because I was a good listener, then he despised me because I listened too much.'

I did a dance around the carpet. 'I think the whole thing's absolutely brilliant. It's my way out of the ghetto! I'm getting used to food. Next it will be clothes. I can't wait. There is a God!'

My mother was just about to warm up some minestrone soup when the phone rang. I raced to the phone in the bedroom while my mother grabbed the receiver in the kitchen. We were both hoping it would be somebody exciting. But it was Grandma Eunice in a rage.

'Where have you been?' she shouted. 'I've been phoning you all evening and your *paying guest* kept on answering. Then he put the answering machine on, just to avoid me. I knew he was there. I can always tell, I'm psychic.'

'He can't come out when he's developing films. Don't take it personally,' my mother stirred the soup with her free hand.

'Frank's gone to Australia! Left this morning!' Eunice said dramatically.

'Gosh, that was quick,' said my mother.

'Yes,' said Eunice ominously. 'And don't you think Jane had a hand to play in that?'

'How could she?'

'All that sex nonsense. I have never been so embarrassed in my life. Frank and I were at an extremely delicate negotiating stage.'

'I'm sorry,' said my mother, automatically accepting the blame.

'It's no good saying sorry. He's gone to Australia!'

'I don't think Jane realised she was going to upset him, did you, Jane?'

Through the bedroom door I could see my mother waving her soup spoon at me to indicate that I should speak up, but I didn't, so my mother waffled on. 'It's been on her mind a lot lately ... I think that's why it came out ... I think she's hoping they might begin to notice her at school if she does this Sex 2000 project. She feels left out.'

Eunice made a small exploding sound. 'Left out! She's left out because she lives in a hovel, and that's all your fault, Louise. You've always looked for the hair shirt.'

My mother waved the soup spoon ever more desperately as she pleaded with me for aid, so I, unwillingly, spoke up.

'Hello, Grandma. Don't worry about Frank going away. I bet he'd booked his ticket ages ago. It's just a coincidence he went the day after your party.'

'Jane,' said Eunice sadly, 'you don't know how things happen in the affairs of the heart. You're too young. How could you talk like that in front of Frank? He was watching you all to see if you passed muster. You've ruined it. It's all over.'

'I'm sure it's not,' I replied. 'I bet he sends you a postcard.'

'I need more than a postcard if I'm going to stay in this house. Cyrus left me with nothing, nothing. I have a mortgage. Women of my age shouldn't have mortgages. Jane, I can't believe that you said all that.'

'Sorry, Grandma.'

'It reflected so badly on me.'

'Sorry, Grandma.'

'When you get to my age opportunities are few and far between.'

'I'm sorry. I won't do it again.'

'And telling him about your nancy boy was the icing on the cake. How could you?'

What was a nancy boy? I looked at my mother and she put her hand over the receiver and mouthed, 'She means Freddy.'

'Do you mean Freddy?' I asked, shocked. My mother cringed. I wasn't meant to confront Grandma Eunice in her grief.

'Frank is a very conservative man,' said Eunice. 'He was brought up in Birmingham. There weren't any nancy boys in Birmingham when he was growing up.'

'Grandma. You mustn't talk like that. It's very prejudiced.'

'Prejudiced!' screamed Eunice. 'How can you talk about

117

prejudice when my life is at stake!'

'But Grandma, Frank will have to change the way he thinks.'

'I can't change Frank. That's the way he is. And I'm heartbroken. If there's the smallest glimmer of hope, if he comes back from Australia, oh dear . . .'

'I'm sure he'll come back," said my mother with absolutely no conviction.

Grandma Eunice let out a small sob, and said, 'If we get another chance, we'll have to show Frank that we can be his sort of family. We'll have to try *very hard* to do things his way. And you know what that means don't you Louise? You must get that man out of your flat.'

'I can't do that!' said my mother, horrified.

'You can do anything you put your mind to. Richard's with me on this. He doesn't think it's good for Jane to have him in the flat.'

My mother gasped. 'He's just making that up. He just wants to make real-estate deals with Frank.'

'And thank God for that! I have a friend in Richard. He's not going to pay Jane's school fees if you don't co-operate and provide her with a good home life.'

'Richard was just here. He didn't say anything about it.'

'Well he couldn't say anything while *that man* was eavesdropping. And he would eavesdrop. Those kind of men do.'

'Freddy doesn't eavesdrop, Grandma,' I said quickly. 'He's not interested in us. He tries to get away from us but we chase him round the flat.'

Eunice ignored me. 'Louise, are you there? What are you going to do about this?'

'Do about it?'

'He will have to go. And Jane will have to stop doing this silly sex thing. It's not good for her. Richard's not paying all that money for her education if she's going to run all over the place asking about sex. You'll have to stop her.'

My mother sighed. 'I don't think I can.'

'You do realise how serious this is don't you?'

There was a long pause and then my mother said in a weak, remote voice, 'I'm sure something good's on the horizon.' It sounded as if she were talking to herself. From my position in the bedroom I could see her moving the soup spoon around the saucepan, with a robotic, low-voltage stirring action.

Grandma Eunice obviously thought this was an irrational reply. 'You need help Louise. I'm your mother and I'm not going to stand by and watch you deteriorate like this. Someone has to do something. I'm going to get you an appointment with a psychiatrist.'

My mother's head sank so low over the saucepan that I thought her face was going to fall into the soup, but at the last moment her head jerked back, she blinked her eyes and looked startled to find herself in the kitchen.

It always took a long time to get Grandma Eunice off the phone but on this occasion it was more of a problem than usual, and the minestrone soup was rather worn out by the time we sat down to it. It was out of a tin but it still tasted very good indeed as we had not eaten for so long.

'You're not going to get rid of Freddy, are you?' I asked.

'Huh?' said my mother.

I wiped my plate and the saucepan with several pieces of brown bread while my mother rinsed her plate and put it in the rack.

'I'm too tired to make anything else,' she said.

'Is that dinner?' I asked in dismay.

'Yes.'

'How can you be so cruel to a starving child?' I asked hungrily.

'I'll make you something tomorrow,' she said, falling on to the sofa and putting her feet up.

'Tomorrow? Tomorrow's no good for me. What kind of mother would let her child go to bed hungry?'

'One who's learning the killer instinct?' she asked.

And she fell asleep, her head sinking back into the feather-loaded cushions.

I rummaged in the cupboard and refrigerator and found that everything required too much effort to prepare, so I ate several bowls of cornflakes with lots of sugar and contemplated the loss of a willing slave. There were disadvantages to this new programme that I had not considered.

SEX 2000 – CONSUMER REPORT

Why would a fourteen-year-old girl want to give someone a blow job?

The girl who played the duke in *Twelfth Night* was called Lydia. It took a lot of courage to approach her because she belonged to one of those extremely snooty groups who thought they were God's ultimate gift to the universe. They were always boasting about how addicted they were to tobacco. When I cornered her in the locker-room after school and asked her why she gave the blow job at the party she said to me, 'Sod off you voyeuristic little twerp!'

I nodded understandingly. I would rather have died than shown her that I was upset. But unfortunately some inner, chinless part of my soul took over and large tear drops, the size of fat peanuts, started plopping down my cheeks at a fast rate. And then, oh hell, my chest started heaving up and down like bellows and I thought now was a good time to shoot myself because I was proving to be exactly like my mother.

Lydia was seriously disgruntled. She looked around to see if she could hand me over to someone and escape, but the locker-room was deserted. 'What's your problem?' she asked.

'Oh nothing,' I heaved.

'Did I say something?'

'No it isn't you.'

It wasn't a complete lie. There were other things disturbing me. Grandma Eunice and Richard were taking it in turns to make increasingly threatening phone calls. There was now deadly serious talk about getting rid of Freddy and there were also heavier demands that I give up my Sex 2000 project. Life was beginning to get to me.

Lydia moved off and looked further afield for help, going out into the corridor and looking up and down, up and down. Then she came back.

'There's no one around.'

'I know,' I heaved and gulped some more.

'Will you be all right if I leave you here?'

'Yes.'

'Well I'm going then.'

'OK.'

She went. I was extremely grateful about that. I had the locker-room to myself and I could let out a big howl.

I was unhappy about losing Freddy. Wherever would we find another lodger who would put such great stuff in our refrigerator and who would understand us so well? And what was the point of asking Lydia to answer my questions for a survey that I would be forced to give up anyway? I was confused. I wailed and wailed.

And then Lydia came back into the locker-room. She stood by the door and stared at me as if I were a cat throwing up.

'Don't worry about it,' I sobbed, hellishly embarrassed. 'Everyone in my family acts like this. We like to cry.'

She ignored that. 'I was in here putting my shoes on, you came in, asked a really crap question, and then you broke down. What did I do?'

'Nothing.'

Her eyes narrowed. 'If you think that crying will make me answer your question then think again.'

'It's nothing to do with that really.'

'Then what is it?'

'Nothing.'

'Look, you're making me miss *Home and Away*. I tell you what. If you shut up right now, I'll agree to a limited interview.'

And that was how I got some really useful insider information. I hiccoughed throughout the interview but otherwise I really did manage to calm down.

'I really appreciate this,' I said, getting out my tape recorder. 'I'm having problems with my boyfriend so it's not an easy subject to research.' I hoped Lydia would not want me to go into detail on this point. My problem with my boyfriend was that there was no boyfriend. I was having a communication problem with my one and only prospect. Obviously a laughable problem as far as she was concerned.

Lydia's eyes narrowed again. 'No names, OK? You'll have to say you talked to an exchange student.'

'OK. Are you ready?'

'I suppose so.'

'You understand that I'm not a person being nosey,' I said, 'I'm like a doctor or a psychiatrist studying a case.'

'If you make any more crap remarks I'm leaving. Just ask the bloody questions.'

'OK, OK, OK. Why did you give him a blow job?'

Lydia, sullen and ill-tempered though she remained, answered as follows: 'Because it was a cool thing to do. Why not?'

'Did you enjoy it?'

'Not really.'

'Did you hate doing it?'

Lydia gave it some careful thought. 'I suppose you could say it gave me a feeling of power.'

'Why did you want a feeling of power?'

'OK. So I didn't want a feeling of power. I did it because it's what people do.'

'Maybe because you've seen it in the movies?'

Lydia shrugged. 'Maybe.'

We both thought about that for a few moments and then Lydia said, 'Right. It could be that. You know there's always a time in every movie when the star's head goes down the screen and out of sight and it's always such a big mystery what she's doing down there. The man's eyes start bulging and the music crescendos. Well now I know.'

'Did you swallow it?'

'Yes.'

'Yuk. Why?'

'Because I didn't know where to put it. I didn't want to be impolite about it.'

'Didn't you feel disgusted?'

'No.'

'Why not?'

'Mental discipline.'

'You're only fourteen. Isn't that too young?'

'Don't be a dork. This is the nineties.'

Conclusion: Mental discipline is important in overcoming lethargy and a desire to puke when you engage in sexual activity. Therefore sex can give weak people strength of character as they fearlessly meet each challenge.

CHAPTER

16

My mother told Freddy that he would have to go.

Her eyes filled with tears as she said, 'I'm sorry, Freddy. I have no choice. Richard says he won't pay Jane's school fees if you don't go. My mother's making my life a misery. They've ganged up together. There's nothing I can do.'

As usual my mother's timing was completely off. Freddy had just come in from a long day on a rainy seashore, tired and starving. He had thrown his photographic equipment down and gone straight to the kitchen to make himself scrambled eggs with chopped bacon bits. He had fried four strips of gammon bacon and chopped them neatly into tiny snippets while I hovered over him and diverted quite a lot of the bacon before it reached the eggs.

'You can't be serious,' he said. And to me he said, 'Keep off, Fatso.'

'Well, yes I am,' said my mother.

'No you're not.' Freddy tipped the scrambled eggs out on to a plate. I grabbed the saucepan and set about eating the substantial amount that was left before he decided on a second helping.

'Why do they want me to go?' he asked.

'Because,' I told him with my mouth crammed with egg, 'My dad says only losers have lodgers.'

He cleared some newspapers from the sofa and sat down with his plate on his lap. 'This place would fall part if I left.'

'And Grandma Eunice doesn't like you having a boyfriend in Winnipeg.'

Freddy took a large forkful of scrambled eggs and then he said icily, 'He's in Ottawa.'

My mother hung her head. 'I'm sorry, Freddy.'

He circled his head to ease out the tensions from his day's work. 'You don't have to be sorry because I'm not going. You can be pushed around by your cretinous relatives as much as you like but I won't be.'

'You're not going?'

'No.'

'Oh.' My mother, looking dismayed, thought about it for a while and then asked, 'What shall I tell them then?'

Freddy took a few more forkfuls of scrambled eggs, pushed the plate to one side and leaned back wearily on the sofa. His eyes were red from battling a cold wind all day.

There was still some scrambled egg left on his plate so I said, 'Shall I wash up the plate Freddy?'

'What were you in a previous life, a vulture?'

My mother asked him again, 'What shall I tell them then?'

'Tell them I'm not going.'

'Oh,' she said.

Dr Jefferies and my mother went off shivering in the icy morning air with puffs of mist swirling out of their mouths and headed in the direction of Hyde Park.

Before she was dragged away my mother whispered to me, 'You'll have to come with us. I won't know what to talk about.'

Dr Jefferies, who had on a fire-engine-red track suit, was loosening up by making little whooshing noises and flapping his arms. 'Let's go,' he said.

'He doesn't want you to talk to him,' I whispered to my mother. 'He's not interested in anything you say.'

'Let's go,' Dr Jefferies repeated.

My mother tugged self-consciously at the cord on her borrowed track suit and hissed in my ear, 'I won't go if you don't come with me.'

'Don't be so neurotic.'

'Let's go for God's sake,' yelled Dr Jefferies, jogging furiously on the spot, like a bull waiting to charge.

And that was that.

My mother attempted a jogging movement, which in her case was a walk with a slight jiggle in it. She kept her head down but I could see an expression close to sheer terror on her face.

Dr Jefferies jogged along side her. 'Now, aggression ... everyone possesses a fixed quantum of aggression, right?' he asked very aggressively.

'Yes,' panted my mother, who had only moved a quarter of an inch.

'Man is, after all, an aggressive animal. Aggression is nice isn't it?'

My mother concentrated on her running and made no reply.

'Isn't it? Say yes,' he barked, or rather snarled, because he showed his excellent white teeth, which were large and flashy and by far his best feature.

'Yes,' said my mother.

'It's nice because it's natural. It's healthy ... healthy, healthy, healthy. Stop hugging yourself. You can't run like that. Throw your chest out. And try moving forward as you run, you'll cover more ground. Now you have as much aggression as er ...' he sought for a suitably aggressive person, '... as me. Right? ... Right?'

'Er ...' my mother panted, 'do I?'

126

'Yes you do. Only in your case, because of this very wasteful compulsion to please everybody, your aggression is turned inwards. Inside you it's like a giant punch-bag. Wham, wham, wham, all day long. You're just a mass of psychic bruises. You're a mess.'

'Yes,' agreed my mother.

I watched until they went round the corner and then I went back into the house with Mrs Moon.

'She's scared because she doesn't want to be left alone with him,' I explained. 'She's a good talker at home but when she's with other people she runs out of conversation.'

Mrs Moon led me into the kitchen. 'I wouldn't worry about it. He's so happy to have her working with him he won't mind what she says. Would you like some hot chocolate?'

'Oh yes please.'

I watched Mrs Moon spoon generous amounts of Cadbury's drinking chocolate into a mug and pour boiling water over it and then plenty of thick creamy milk from a bottle. Such a change from the skimmed milk in impenetrable cartons my mother bought.

'Dr Jefferies doesn't seem all that happy to be working with my mother,' I said, probing.

Mrs Moon slapped the hot chocolate down on the table. Then she set about getting herself into the kitchen armchair, as I'd seen her do once before, by easing herself down on it slowly and then midway dropping into a dangerous free fall. 'That's because he's got a bad temper,' she said upon landing. 'But the truth is he's desperate to keep your mother doing this course. Desperate.'

'Really?'

'Oh yes. His publisher came to lunch and said they couldn't publish his new book, the one he's working on now, because ...'

127

Mrs Moon patted her 1940s hair roll into place and furrowed her brow.

'... Now let me see. Why was it? It was something to do with the rats. I think he talked about the rats too much, yes that was it. The publisher told Dr Jefferies that he needed a human being. He said human beings would sell the book. Yes that's what he said. Rats don't sell books.'

'You mean my mother's story will sell the book?'

'They're hoping.' Mrs Moon shook her head doubtfully. 'Well ... you've got to have hope, haven't you.'

'And Dr Jefferies is desperate?'

'Desperate.'

'So he's *got* to teach my mother the killer instinct?'

'If he wants to get his book published. And he really cares about his books. He gets very touchy about them. I think he would chop my head off if I lost one old envelope with some little note scratched on it. I have to watch what I do.'

'Aren't you scared of him?'

'Well I have my work to do. There's no point in getting scared. He complains all the time because he doesn't want anyone around.'

'Why?'

'I don't know. Originally he asked me to come two mornings a week. But I can't get everything done in that time. This is a big place. Someone has to keep it going.'

Mrs Moon supplied me with toast and Marmite and another cup of hot chocolate, while we sat in the steaming warmth and forgot about my mother staggering pitifully along icy pathways in the park.

When she came back, and slumped over the kitchen table, my mother had very pink cheeks and pink hands. I expect her entire body was pink because it seemed to be in shock from so much exercise.

Dr Jefferies was also a ruddy colour. My mother told me

later that he had run three times as far as she had, running up and down the path like an enthusiastic poodle, while she tried to maintain a movement that could be identified as jogging.

'The trick is,' he told my mother, as he wrenched off his brilliant red track suit top to reveal a striped T-shirt, 'not to run too fast to begin with. Allow your lungs to get used to taking in the extra oxygen.'

My mother looked at him mutely.

'You're right,' he said, as if he now understood my mother's silent language, 'I'm talking to myself. You were going so slowly you were practically standing still. You were overtaken by old ladies with walking sticks.'

Mrs Moon intervened. 'I saw her go off down the road, she wasn't that bad.'

'Who the hell asked you Mrs Moon? And what are you doing here? It's Tuesday.'

Mrs Moon shrugged and went over to the stove and started rubbing it with a cloth.

Dr Jefferies stared at her hunched shoulders and broad back. He was obviously contemplating a nasty confrontation but decided against it and turned to my mother instead. 'OK. That's it. We'll do that three mornings a week. Get you in shape. Get the blood going. And I want you back here tomorrow night.'

My mother's eyes instantly showed more than the usual amount of alarm.

'What's the matter?' asked Dr Jefferies.

'I can't come tomorrow,' breathed my mother.

'Why not?'

My mother opened her mouth and left it at half-mast.

Dr Jefferies became very irritable. He started kicking his foot against the table leg, obviously as a substitute for kicking Mrs Moon and my mother. Then in desperation he turned to me. 'Why can't she come tomorrow?'

'She's going to see Dr Bloomfield. She's a psychiatrist my father recommended.'

I could see a surge of adrenalin run through Dr Jefferies. He used it to kick the table a few more times, not in a wildly aggressive way, but it was certainly more than a tap with his foot.

'You're seeing me,' he said in steady, controlled tones. 'You don't go anywhere else. I'm enough. And you certainly don't cancel one of my sessions to see some psychiatrist I've never heard of.'

'Huh,' said my mother.

'I want you here tomorrow night at seven-thirty. Do you understand that?'

'Huh,' said my mother.

Dr Jefferies picked up his track suit top and wiped his face with it. 'That's understood then. See you tomorrow.' And he walked out of the kitchen.

SEX 2000 – CONSUMER REPORT

Does sexual attraction prevent proper functioning of the brain?

I asked Freddy who, sensing that he was just about to be grilled, sunk into the armchair and rattled his *Evening Standard* authoritatively.

'Freddy, do you totally lose your head when you're around certain people?'

The phone rang and the answering machine whirred into action. It was Grandma Eunice again, demanding to know why my mother had not attended her appointment with Dr Bloomfield. Freddy kept his head bent over his paper. I could see by the way his mouth was set that he was determined not to be bothered by either the phone or me. But I had to ask someone about this important sexual topic, so I persisted.

'Garvie and I have had two conversations now and I've talked gibberish both times. They weren't real conversations anyway. Garvie brought Vincent's towels into the launderette and I said, "Do you like water?" Can you believe that? *Do you like water?* And then when he came back to pick them up I told him the soap powder was part dandruff. *Part dandruff!* When he's there I don't act like myself. I become a totally different person.'

'Uh huh,' said Freddy.

'Like yesterday, he was in the office when I went in. And my heart started going THUMP THUMP. And before I knew it I was showing him how to shake free Pepsis out of the dispenser.'

'Uh huh. Where's your mother?'

'She's gone to her evening class with Dr Jefferies. You know! That's why Grandma Eunice keeps on phoning.'

'Oh right.' Freddy made a face and returned to his paper.

'Do you feel persecuted, Freddy?'

'By you?'

'No. Not by me! By Grandma Eunice.'

'I've got better things to do than to think about that old bag.'

'She's not very appreciative of all your generosity.'

'I'm not generous. Stupid maybe.'

'I thought those orange-cream-filled chocolate biscuits you got yesterday were amazing.'

'Uh huh. I wouldn't know. I haven't had one yet.'

'Well take my word for it, they're incredible. But Freddy, can you explain why I would do such a dangerous thing right in front of Dolores? I mean she was right there in the office.'

'What dangerous thing?'

'I just told you! I showed Garvie how to shake a free Pepsi out of the dispenser. Dolores was about three metres away, and I was kicking and shaking the machine, making a hell of a noise. And all because he was there. I wasn't myself.'

'Uh huh.'

'Have you ever gone completely mad because of another person?'

'On occasions.' Freddy turned to the television page.

'And did you do something like that?'

'Like what?'

I was exasperated. 'Like stealing two Pepsis. Just to show off. *Please*, Freddy. I'm racing against time now. They're trying to stop me from doing this project.'

'You shouldn't steal.'

'It wasn't really stealing. Vincent's swindling my mother, he doesn't give her a proper wage, so I thought it was fair really. It didn't make up for what he owes her.'

'Uh huh.'

'But I was out of my mind to do it while Dolores was there. Do you know what saved me?'

'What?'

'She was on the phone and she'd broken her nail. Her nails are decorated with gold flowers and she has a major conniption every time she breaks one.'

'Uh huh.'

'So she was really distracted. But you should have seen Garvie's face! He was really scared. He knows Vincent could explode over something like that and she's like his major spy. She tells him everything. I was just getting the second Pepsi out when she looked up and said, "What's all that noise?" And I said, "The machine got stuck." And she believed me!'

'Uh huh.'

'And I gave Garvie the Pepsi and he said thank you. And then he ran out of things to say and he went out. But what I want to know is, how long will this go on?'

'How long will what go on?'

'How long will I go on being this totally mad person when I'm around Garvie?'

Freddy looked up from the magazine. 'I haven't a clue.'

Conclusion: Sexual attraction prevents proper functioning of the brain. This would explain all the really ridiculous mistakes that are constantly being made all over the world.

CHAPTER

17

My mother returned from her evening session with Dr Jefferies looking more resolute than I had ever seen her look before. She threw her three-ringed killer instinct folder on to the kitchen counter with a definitely rebellious air. *What progress*, I thought.

'That's it,' she declared. 'I'm never going back to that man again. He's rude, abusive and bad-tempered. He never gives me the benefit of the doubt. I'm sick of it.'

She marched around the living-room picking up stray books, plates, apple cores and soda cans that Freddy and I had left lying around.

'What did he say?' I asked.

Freddy strolled out of his room holding his new CamLink video editor and watched my mother curiously. Another first. He never came out to watch anything.

My mother stuffed all the old newspapers forcefully into a Safeway plastic bag. 'He said I shouldn't feel guilty about my daughter. And that I wouldn't learn the killer instinct while I was successfully manufacturing all this guilt.'

She threw the bag into a kitchen cupboard and began picking up items of clothing – socks, sweatshirts, and shoes that Freddy and I had discarded while we watched television. 'He said that I'd raised you in the worst way possible, that I've never frustrated you and you think you're omnipotent and that you'll get a big shock when you go out into the world and find out you're an ordinary human being.'

I gasped with annoyance. 'What absolute codswallop.'

'He said I had to analyse my love for my child. That permissive love isn't the only kind there is. He said there's aggressive love. That if I really loved my child I wouldn't give into its every whim.'

'*Its* whim? He called me an *it*?' I was extremely indignant about that.

'And he's lascivious. Bad-tempered and lascivious.' My mother sat down on the sofa with a collection of abandoned socks on her lap and looked around at the tidier room. It was shabby but had character. There were a couple of good brass lamps left over from my father's brass obsession days, heavy velvet curtains donated by the previous flat owner and a grey carpet well cleaned by my mother, who never let a smudge lurk on its surface.

'Is lascivious like lecherous?' I was hazy on the finer points of vocabulary in those days, as I may have mentioned before.

'Sort of,' said my mother.

Freddy sat down on the sofa next to my mother and rested the video editor on his knee. 'Lecherous is a little further up the scale than lascivious. Like lascivious is amateur, lecherous is professional.'

'Don't worry,' I said to my mother. 'He's not going to rape you.'

Freddy agreed. 'He's definitely not going to rape you. Well – if he did rape you then he'd ask you to pay him for it.'

My mother's eyes opened wide. 'He wouldn't would he?' Her pale, thin face turned first to Freddy then to me for reassurance.

'Oh yes,' said Freddy. 'He'd definitely want repayment.'

'No he wouldn't. He needs you for his book,' I said, reminding her once more about our ace card. 'He can't get it published if he doesn't have you to experiment on. You're a free guinea-pig. He should pay *you*.'

Freddy looked extremely dubious about that. 'My advice to you is don't bring sex into it. He'll be looking for compensation. He'll be round here expecting free meals. Don't come begging me to make him Eggs Benedict.'

My mother's anguish increased. 'Eggs Benedict?'

'How is he lascivious?' I asked, wanting details. 'What does he do?'

'Has he laid his hands on any part of your anatomy?' asked Freddy.

My mother looked horrified. 'Oh no!' She ran her fingers through her hair, which was looking neglected and stringy. 'He said he'd like to see my legs.'

'You're kidding,' I said.

'No I'm not,' she said, looking hurt. 'He said I always wear trousers and he'd like me to wear a skirt.'

Freddy and I gazed studiously at my mother's legs, well wrapped as they were in a thick, brown tweedy material.

'He's saying that to bolster your ego. It's part of the programme,' Freddy explained.

The phone on the table by the sofa rang and my mother jumped. 'It's only Grandma Eunice,' I said, as the answering machine picked up the call. The sound was turned down but a tiny, angry voice could be heard leaving an irate message.

'Talk to her,' ordered Freddy, who was now beginning to turn his interest back to his new video editor. 'You're going to have to deal with her sooner or later.'

'Do I have to?' asked my mother.

'Don't you feel stronger, more able to cope?' I asked hopefully. 'Haven't you got a small touch of the killer instinct?'

'How on earth could I?' she complained bitterly. 'All he does is shout at me and tell me that being British is bad for my health.'

Freddy stood up and headed towards his room. 'Talk to her. She'll break the bloody phone if she rings any more. For a start tell her to stop phoning. It's harassment.'

'You said, "For a *start* tell her to *stop*,"' I smirked. I used to find that sort of thing funny in those days.

Freddy gave me a withering look. For quite some time he had been trying to upgrade my sense of humour. He looked at my mother who was staring intensely at her knees. 'Your mother is a mystery. She's so pathetic she's scary.' He turned back, leaned over the sofa and grabbed the phone. 'Just one moment,' he said authoritatively to Eunice, 'will you hold?'

And he began humming the theme from 'A Man and a Woman' to provide phone waiting music while he thrust the receiver into my mother's hands.

My mother caught the receiver like someone playing pass the parcel. I scooted out of the way before she could pass it to me and Freddy ducked behind the sofa and retired to his room. I went to listen on the phone in the bedroom as I had to observe how well the killer instinct instruction was working.

'Hello,' said my mother falteringly.

'Louise!' exploded Grandma Eunice. 'What is going on? Dr Bloomfield phoned Richard and said you hadn't turned up.'

'I'm sorry.'

'You're sorry! That appointment was *very* important. Why on earth didn't you go and see her?'

'I'm sorry. It couldn't be avoided. I had another engagement.'

'Another engagement. Couldn't you have cancelled it?'

'I tried but he wouldn't listen.'

137

'Who wouldn't listen?'

'Dr Jefferies.'

'That American?'

'Yes.'

'You chose to go to that phony American rather than a decent British psychiatrist?'

'He got very annoyed when I tried to cancel.'

'Well of course he would, wouldn't he. Americans are loud-mouthed and cocky. They're common. They have no education, they learn everything from the television. You can't put yourself into the hands of a barbarian like that.'

'Sorry.'

'Sorry. What do you mean sorry? Are you going to stop seeing this man?'

'I'm going to try.'

'Trying isn't enough. I tell you, Louise, you can't put yourself into the hands of an American. They don't know anything. All they have in their country are petrol stations and motels. They don't know anything about architecture. And they have absolutely no self-control. They all have guns and they shoot them at the drop of a hat. The whole country's a war zone. They're sick people. There's absolutely no way an American can give you any help. I want you to see Dr Bloomfield. She'll sort you out. And Louise! Was that your rent boy who answered the phone?'

'It was Freddy.'

'Have you given him his notice?'

'Yes.'

'When's he going?'

'He didn't say.'

'It's not up to him to say. *You* tell him Louise.'

'All right.'

Grandma Eunice nattered on for ages after that but I gave up listening in. Her voice was beginning to sound like the really unpleasant screeching noise made by Freddy's electric juicer on its highest speed.

When my mother finally put the phone down she looked drained. 'I'm being ground to death by everyone,' she said, with a deathly face. Her skin had turned a sort of oatmeal shade, the same colour as the cushions around her.

I looked at her disappointedly. 'When you first came in I thought you'd learned a bit of the killer instinct. But I can see now that you haven't learned anything.'

'No I haven't,' she said gloomily. 'I have no choice. I will have to kill myself.'

I gasped with horror. 'That's a terrible thing to say in front of your child. Children of my age are very impressionable.'

She stuck her chin out, sulky and resentful. 'We talked about it before.'

'Only in jest.'

'Well what am I going to do?'

'You've got to learn the killer instinct. You've *got* to learn it.'

'Jane, you're dreaming. I'll never change. People don't change. Dr Jefferies just shouts at me. Nothing's going to happen.'

She lifted herself slowly from the couch and went off in a death-walk to the bedroom.

'Well don't kill yourself,' I shouted. 'I won't allow it. I'll stay awake all night and watch you like a hawk.'

'All right, All right. I won't do it tonight. Relax.'

She said 'relax' with an American accent. I had heard Dr Jefferies use that word on several occasions. It was an American term for 'belt up you're boring me', and my mother said it in that same irritated, insulting way he said it. I took it as a small glimmer of hope. If she could pick up one of his expressions, who knew what else she could pick up? There *had* to be hope.

SEX 2000 – CONSUMER REPORT

Question – For peace of mind, success and
happiness, how much time of the day should you
devote to thinking about sex?

'My life is dire,' I told Sophia, as we changed for our tennis lesson. 'My grandmother's been phoning the school complaining about my project and my mother's going to kill herself.'

'Oh Jane, you poor thing.' Sophia tugged at strands of her long hair which were caught inside her sport's shirt.

'I'm trying to stay positive but it's hard.' I laced up my worn trainers and hoped the teacher wouldn't complain about my toes protruding through holes.

'You mustn't let life get you down.'

'No, I suppose not.'

'Sophia picked up her racket and headed towards the courts. 'What did you want to ask me about?'

'Oh yes. It's about happiness. I thought a cheerful question might cheer us up. For peace of mind, success and happiness, how much time of the day should you devote to thinking about sex?'

Sophia thought about it as a light rain began to fall. 'It's *very* important. I'd say you have to think about it at least seventy-five per cent of the day.'

I was awed that it would require that much thought. 'Sophia, do you think about it *that* much?'

'Not yet,' she replied, 'but I'm working on it.'

Conclusion: Sex is vital for your health and well-being. Sometimes your mind may wander away from thoughts of sex if you are not careful. But those who are determined to achieve peace of mind, success and happiness will overcome this mental obstacle.

CHAPTER
18

'I want an interim report on your project next week, Jane. I want to know *exactly* what you're doing.'

Mrs Cassels leaned against her desk in her slate-grey knitted coat, and faced the class with that look in her eye that she always had when looking at us collectively, a slight repulsion, a slight wish that she could get away. She had taught in a state school before coming to teach us, and thought state pupils were more 'real' than us, the over-indulged, over-educated and over-privileged results of fee paying.

'Interim?' I asked. 'How long is that?' I had no idea what an interim report was and looked around the class to see if anyone could explain. But they were too busy making the usual elaborate time-wasting preparations, searching lengthily for the perfect pens and pencils, and making archeological digs for textbooks.

'Bring me what you've written so far. I want to see all of it.'

When I sat down Sophia snickered in her usual superior way and said, 'Gutted!'

'It's not funny, Sophia,' I complained. 'She wants an interim. This is the end. They'll take it away from me.'

'What's an interim?'

'I just asked her that. She said it means everything you've done.'

'Then why didn't she say everything you've done?' asked Sophia as she helped herself to my best fountain pen.

'Because she's a teacher.'

'Well you never really wanted to do this project anyway.'

'True,' I sniffed, 'but I've got used to it. I really don't want to give it up now. Sex is very addictive.'

Garvie turned up at Vincent's Coachworks and Launderette with a friend, a fat, talkative boy called Andy in flared jeans and a black leather jacket. Andy had one and a half double chins; they did not seem to trouble him at all, and if they did, he kept it very well disguised.

He came over to talk to me almost immediately, which made a refreshing change from the monosyllabic Garvie, who was always hiding in the workshop.

'Why are you working in this dump?' he asked, chewing gum and trying to look very street. He had a London accent.

'I need the money,' I said coolly. I think it came across as cool. I wished I wasn't wearing the dreaded pink overall. Then I asked, 'What school do you go to?'

I had an instinct this would be a crushing question. He tried to fob me off by saying, 'Same as Garvie.'

'What's that?'

'Oh, a school,' he said casually. 'They're all the same, what's the difference?'

I smelled a rat. It took quite some time before he admitted that he and Garvie went to a public school. It was hard to be accepted as a lad if you went to a gits' school. The highways and byways of London were full of boys talking in tough city accents and wearing street cred studs and denims who had a secret other life at a poncey public school.

It certainly was an Achilles' heel for Andy and he

142

stumbled quite a bit trying to get round that but then he got back on his feet. He was a real talker. He could have been a disc jockey, no problem, and I enjoyed communicating with a real live boy. Communication with Garvie had been so slight I was not sure it would be accepted as such by those who were expert on such matters. I felt at last that I really had broken through on to the opposite shore, that island where they kept all those illusive males.

'Have you come to get a job here?' I asked him.

This was yet another area he was cagey about.

'No-o,' he answered. It was easy to see that his mind was running over a lot of possible replies because he was on the transparent side. He finally chose, 'I wouldn't want to work in a dump like this. Garvie says he gets paid shit.'

'He gets paid more than me,' I protested.

'Well he's a guy,' said Andy, just to be annoying. Judging from this sample male before me I could see that boys were just like girls, except they seemed to be less devious. Everything was up front.

After we'd had a quick row about equal rights, Andy said, 'So what do you think of Garvie?'

'He's OK,' I answered carefully.

'Just OK?'

'Why?'

'I just wondered,' he said, kicking a stone and looking around for something bigger. 'Don't get your knickers in a twist.'

'What a terrible cliché,' I said.

Andy paused to study me. 'Are you always like this?'

'Like what?'

'You act like an old lady.'

'I don't.'

'Yes you do. I don't know what Garvie sees in you personally.'

This was a bombshell. Garvie saw something in me! He had given me some thought! Ring out wild bells!

Andy was now kicking one of Vincent's prize pieces of automobile around the gravel. It was some sort of vital engine part, left to wait its turn with all the other pieces in the alley. I watched the mini soccer display while I tried to gather my thoughts. What on earth was I expected to say after a remark like that?

The talker didn't wait, thank goodness. If only all boys were like Andy, I could have had a life of easy-listening stretching out before me, nodding occasionally to show I was awake, giving the odd smile, and never worrying about what to say, never finding myself dribbling on maniacally about nothing in particular. Life would have been a breeze.

'So,' said Andy, 'would you go out with him if he asked?'

'With Garvie?'

'Who else, you nit?'

'Where is he?' I didn't dare turn my head to see if Garvie was looking.

'He's waiting for a report.' Andy booted the obscure engine part towards a bucket with great force and it crashed against the side with a satisfying wallop, making tinny echoing noises up and down the alley.

'Is that why you came?' I asked him in a very little voice. I was beginning to sound really wet.

'You ask a lot of nosey questions.'

'Do I?' Wetter still. Maybe conversation was easy with Andy but to say it was a breeze was probably an exaggeration. I was beginning to discover that nothing in life was ever all that easy where men were concerned.

'Yes you do. So what's your answer?'

'What was the question?' As if I didn't know.

'Bloody hell. The question was, would you go out with Garvie if he asked?'

'Sure, why not?'

'OK. So it's a deal?'

'Yes.'

'Thank God for that.'

And Andy turned and went off kicking another engine part into oblivion. He returned five minutes later to ask for my phone number which I felt-tipped on to a crisp packet.

I hardly saw Garvie for the rest of the day. I caught glimpses of him dashing hither and yon with an intensity I considered quite unnecessary for Vincent's Coachworks. He reminded me of my mother. Why would anyone be intense when working for Vincent?

When I engineered it so that we would come face to face outside the workshop, he kept his head down and said, 'Thanks for the phone number.' Then he wriggled past me like a cat trying to get out of the front door.

Like a very small hazelnut in a giant nutcracker, manipulated by Dr Jefferies on one side and Grandma Eunice and Richard on the other, my mother was helpless and, as would be expected, very squeezed. Giving up the killer instinct lessons would have scored many Brownie points with Eunice and Richard. It seemed the best way out. But in order to look Dr Jefferies in the eye and tell him she was not taking any more of his lessons she needed – she needed the killer instinct.

How difficult in the scale of human endeavour was it to look Dr Jefferies in the eye and say, 'I've had enough'?

For my mother it was too difficult even to contemplate. She just about managed the idea of a resignation letter. 'I'll write it,' she said trepidatiously, 'and you can put it through his letter-box.'

'Why can't *you* put it through his letter-box?' I asked indignantly.

'Jane!' whined my mother. 'I can't go up to his letter-box. He might see me through the window.'

'Do you think Dr Jefferies is the sort of man who stands at the window peeping through the curtains?'

'You can never tell with anybody what they do when they're alone.'

We had this conversation many times throughout this period of deadlock but it always ended up with my refusal to deliver the letter.

Why not post the letter?

Because she had a killer instinct session every day and my mother was mentally incapable of facing Dr Jefferies during the delicate interval *after* she had posted the letter but *before* it had arrived.

'The letter would be written all over my face,' she moaned. And I had to agree with her. Deception was something completely outside my mother's grasp. It was astounding to me that one person could be incapable of so many things. How could she have survived on this earth without lying at least once?

Her only hope now was to avoid Eunice and Richard until she had at least a smattering of killer instinct. She avoided them by being out. This was not difficult. The killer instinct lessons took up more and more of her time until eventually she only came home to sleep.

New lessons included judo, which left her as befuddled as the karate, and boxing sessions where she was required to rain blows on a punch-bag. Pencil portraits of her enemies were pinned on to the punch-bag and she was expected to supply violent smashes to the smiling faces or punch-bag bellies of Vincent, Grandma Eunice, Richard and the workmen in the alley.

She was repeatedly taken over assault courses where she had to scale brick walls, swing on ropes and cross swirling

146

rivers by means of a thin tree trunk. It was meant to teach her physical courage but she invariably came home wet, muddy and defeated. And of course there were long 'psychological sessions' as my mother called them, where she was required to discuss her childhood, re-enact various difficult scenes from her developing years and to act out future 'problem situations' that she might have to face.

The acting out of these scenes was excruciatingly painful for my mother, largely because Dr Jefferies played all the enemy roles and he did them so badly. He would prance about like a pantomime dame doing his interpretation of bossy Eunice and expect my mother to take him seriously, while she struggled with the trauma of handling a woman who had manipulated and squelched her since birth.

'It's absolute murder,' my mother complained, 'to have one autocrat pretending to be another autocrat.'

I was not quite sure of the meaning of autocrat. Did it have something to do with cars? Whatever it meant, it obviously described a shared characteristic of Grandma Eunice and Dr Jefferies. So I felt I was right in saying, 'They're only autocrats when they're around you. You bring out the autocrat in everyone.'

I now know that autocrat means 'a ruler with absolute power or any domineering self-willed person', so I think that was an extremely deft and incisive thing to say.

After six weeks of instruction there was no visible change in my mother. I watched her closely but she still seemed to be the same disastrously over-sensitive weakling that she had always been, until one evening Freddy came into the kitchen and said, 'What's wrong with your mother?'

'Why?' I asked.

'Can't you hear her? She's in the bathroom.'

I went to the bathroom door, which had no lock, and opened it a small chink. My mother was sitting on the loo singing loudly and very determinedly, 'We shall overcome'.

I went back to Freddy, overjoyed. 'It's a breakthrough!' I cried.

Freddy ran his hands through his ripe-blackberry hair. 'One person's breakthrough is another person's mental breakdown.'

'Oh.'

I had to go away and think about that.

SEX 2000 – CONSUMER REPORT

Question – What does a man expect when he has a date with a woman?

Vincent eventually ran out of things to pretend to be doing and gave in. He picked his way through the car debris in the alley and sat down heavily on a pile of tyres, causing the seams of his overalls, which were straining to hold in his expanding flesh, to lose a few more stitches. 'All right, what is this? Desert Island Discs?'

I had come round to the garage after school. As it was a weekday and Dolores was not around, my mother was in the office. I could see her anxious face peering over the counter as I tried to find a place next to Vincent on the tyres. He had not left much room for me so I knelt on the gravel in front of him and switched on my tape recorder.

'I would like to ask you, as an experienced male, what do you expect when you go out on a date with a woman?'

'Sex. What else?'

'What is sex?'

'What is sex?'

'Yes, what is sex?'

Vincent scratched a bald part of his head and looked up and down the alley as if he were watching a ghost go by on a motorbike. 'You don't know what sex is? You want me to tell you what it is?'

'I want you to tell me what you think it is. Freddy said sex is life.'

'Oh . . . you want an arty farty definition. I can do that.'

'OK then.'

'Let me see . . . what is sex?'

'What is it?'

'I'm thinking. I'm thinking.' He watched the ghost ride up and down a couple of times.

'There's only ten minutes left on this tape.'

'Don't rush me . . . OK. How's this? Sex is the most powerful force known to man, greater than the atomic bomb.' He looked up in triumph, tickled pink with himself, and grinned like someone who had just given a brilliant answer.

'So why is it so powerful?' I asked.

'Why is it so powerful? It's powerful because men will kill for it. They'll climb mountains for it. They'll die for it.'

'Would you die for it?'

The grin went. 'Personally – no. Because the way I look at it, you've always got motorbikes.' He meant the kind without ghosts on them. He had three motorbikes, which he constantly took apart and put together, and when one of them was put together, he rode it along the motorway and showed off his tattoos.

'If you wouldn't die for it, what would you do to get it?'

'I don't have to do anything for it. I've never had a problem with women making themselves available when I want it. Because what you'll learn, sweetheart, is that women are always on the lookout for men, which is sex. I mean, what else are men? Why do women hang around pubs? For the beer? Oh no. You wait. In a year you'll be like all the others, hanging around, breathing heavy, waiting to catch some poor bastard.'

'Actually, I'm just about to have a date. That's why I'm asking you for this information.'

'Well there you go. You've already started.'

'Why do you think women are always on the lookout for sex?'

'How should I know? That's the way it is. Women are hungry for it. Men provide it. They'll tell you it's the other way round but it's not. There's a lot of needy women out there and I've always done my best to help them out. I mean, I'm being frank here. You asked me so I'm telling you. You're old enough now. You're going out on dates. You'll be leaping on some poor unsuspecting bloke.'

I looked down the list on my clipboard and found the next question. 'Is sex worth the effort you put into it?'

'How do you mean is it worth it?' The question annoyed him.

'I mean, do you ever think you could have done something better or is it always the best thing to do?'

Vincent lifted his chest and took a big intake of breath. 'I can't speak for everyone,' he said seriously. 'But for myself – any woman that spends some time with me will never think she could have done something better. Sublime is the word for it. Waves of ecstasy, followed by mountains, tidal waves. It's indescribable.'

'I suppose that's great if you're into ecstasy.'

He picked up a nail and threw it scornfully at the office window, where it clinked and made my mother jump. 'No one's into ecstasy. You can't be into it. Ecstasy hits you. You're helpless. You'll be helpless. You'll see. You'll be a slave to it. The world's a slave to it.'

'You can't opt out?' I asked.

'No you can't. If you do, you go funny, you get twisted. You have to give into it or else you'll start chewing your nightgown or torturing rabbits.'

150

A customer came to collect his Citroën and my interviewee was totally distracted. When he came back down the alley, I tried to get a few more minutes of Vincent spouting forth about sexual ecstasy on my tape recorder but he had lost interest. I had been prepared for this because I knew he had a very short attention span.

I tried though. 'Vincent, please. Just two more questions.'

I followed him over to the office. One of his favourite occupations was to force a free can out of the drinks dispenser. (This is how I had learned how to do it myself.) It appealed to his delinquent side, even though he was stealing from himself. By a combination of fiddling, kicking and shaking, he enticed a lemonade out. 'Howzatt!' he called triumphantly.

He took the contraband can and tried to fit his wide rear end on to a narrow window ledge. My mother was hunched over the counter buried in invoices, trying to be invisible as usual.

'Did you know your daughter's been asking me about sex?'

'Yes,' said my mother, without looking up.

He took a swig from his can. 'Don't you find that a little perverted? I mean she's getting a fancy education learning Latin and Greek and all she can do is go around talking dirty.'

'Her intentions are good.'

'You don't mind her going around being perverted as long as her intentions are good?'

My mother didn't answer that.

Vincent took another swig. 'That's a dangerous philosophy, you know that? Like you could have someone going around dropping their children off high buildings and you'd say that it was all right as long as their intention was good.'

'That's not the same,' said my mother quietly.

We all three knew that Vincent was going to stay there making a nuisance of himself until he'd emptied his can of lemonade. That was how he entertained himself. He liked to torment my mother and she was too polite to do anything about it.

So, to the rescue again, I switched on my tape recorder and said, 'One more question.'

He raised his eyebrows. 'See, what did I tell you? She can't leave it alone.'

'What advice do you have to give me about sex?' I asked.

'Advice?' Vincent looked over at my mother and grinned suggestively. 'I'm a man. There's only one piece of advice a man can give a woman about sex. Get your—'

'She means mature advice,' my mother said quickly.

'If it's mature, it's not sex, it's something else.'

I put my tape recorder right under his nose. 'Your remarks are being immortalised on tape.'

He threw his can into a bin. 'Advice. OK. I'd tell them sex is a great gift. Don't screw it up.' He cackled and eased his capacious rear off the window sill. 'Sorry, girls. Got to love you and leave you.'

Conclusion: A man expects sex when he goes out on a date with a woman. He expects a woman to expect the same thing. As some inexperienced people don't like sex as much as they should, it might be advisable to take a secret ballot at the beginning of the evening to avoid disappointment and unnecessary expense.

CHAPTER
19

My upcoming date with Garvie was filling me with fear and anxiety. I really wasn't enjoying life any more. Everything I looked at or thought of reminded me that, in a few short days, I would be thrown into a bewildering sexual cauldron, churned around, gasping for air, drowning in libidinous expectations. Theory and practice seemed a universe apart. How could any human being do the things that I'd been writing about in my reports? How could Garvie and I do any of those things? I would rather die first. But I would rather die first than let anyone knew that I would rather die first. I didn't want to be left out in the cold. I wanted to join the human race. I had a reputation to keep, or rather, to start.

Would he want one of those heavy three-course-meal kisses I'd seen everyone exchanging at the charity ball? And what on earth would we talk about? Sophia had told me that, as Garvie could not talk, he would resort to sex right away.

'Men who can't think of anything to say just put their hands in your knickers,' she told me.

The idea seemed horribly invasive. I looked upon my knickers as peaceful garments, useful and comfortable. I didn't want a tobacco-stained, inky hand with dirty finger-nails anywhere near them.

Sophia had absolutely no patience with my concern. 'It's not politically correct to think that your knickers preserve a sacred area. You can't indulge yourself in that kind of thinking, Jane. Get with it. This is the warm, giving nineties.'

I cornered Freddy when he was chaining his bicycle to the railings outside our flat.

'Freddy, I have pains in my stomach as soon as I think about going out with Garvie. What shall I do?'

Freddy pushed his rusty padlock into place and then removed the saddle from the bike. 'He's not a monster,' he said, putting the saddle into his equipment bag. 'You should never be scared of a fellow human being.'

I followed Freddy (wearing his photographer's uniform of black leather jacket and Levis) down the steps to our front door. 'You wouldn't say that about Hitler,' I said.

Freddy stepped inside the front door and sniffed. He always checked the air as smells were easily trapped in our small quarters and he was constantly complaining about bad cabbage odours. 'We're not talking about Hitler, this is a thirteen-year-old kid,' he said, after satisfying himself that any odour was within bearable limits.

'He's fourteen.'

'Oh my God!' Freddy slammed the door behind him. 'He's ancient. You'll need a suit of armour. You'll need a tank!'

'Freddy! You're not being helpful. This is serious.' I trooped after him as he went into the kitchen, always his first port of call.

'I *am* being serious. Have you thought that he could be just as scared as you?' He opened the refrigerator door and gazed inside it for inspiration.

'Yes. I've considered that. But what do I do when he stops being scared?'

He closed the refrigerator door without having been

inspired to select anything and went to a cabinet where we kept biscuits and crackers. 'Look, why don't you ask him over here? Then you'll have two great big adult chaperones.'

'Chaperones! Nobody has chaperones.'

'OK,' he said, and closed the cabinet door, as I had pretty well finished off anything worth eating there. 'So where are you going?'

'We're going to see a film.'

Freddy returned to the refrigerator and opened it again. 'All right. Tell me what the film is. I'll buy a ticket and sit in the row behind you.' He selected some pitta bread and hummus. 'If he tries anything too heavy-handed I'll come leaping over the seat and say, "Jane! How are you? Do you remember me from the church jumble sale?"'

'If you did that I'd kill you.'

He put the pitta bread into the toaster. 'Then take a friend with you.'

'Who? Sophia? If she came with a boy they'd be so busy getting off they wouldn't know I existed.'

'I've got it. Tabasco sauce!'

'What?'

'If he comes on too strong you squirt tabasco sauce at him.'

A bottle of ancient tabasco sauce, its label stained with repeated dribblings, was produced from its hiding place behind dusty vinegar and Worcestershire sauce bottles. He poured a drop on to a spoon. 'Taste it.'

With considerable caution I put my tongue into the spot of pinky brown watery liquid. Instantly my tongue was aflame. It was worse than hydrochloric acid. It was a liquid that could dissolve bones and skin. 'Freddy! That's disgusting!' I rushed to get a glass of water.

Freddy looked triumphant. 'That's it. The ultimate weapon.'

*

To stave off panic I went round to Dr Jefferies' house and sat in the kitchen with Mrs Moon while my mother had her evening session upstairs.

'What was it like when you went out on your first date?' I asked her.

Mrs Moon patted her well-coiffed 1940s hair and thought back into the far reaches of time. 'It was raining. We went to a whelk stall, but I didn't like whelks.'

'Did he try anything?'

'Try anything?'

'Anything sexual.'

Mrs Moon drew a breath. 'Oh no. Not at a whelk stall. Oh no. We were very young. I went home to my mother.'

I had obviously offended her. So I changed the subject. 'How's Dr Jefferies getting on with the lessons? Is he pleased with my mother?'

'The publisher phoned yesterday,' Mrs Moon said solemnly, and picked her knitting out of a tapestry bag. She was making a pullover in stout green wool. 'From New York, long distance. He said he didn't think Dr Jefferies could pull it off in time for publication.'

I didn't ask her how she knew what the publisher said on the phone. I was certain that Dr Jefferies never told her anything except 'go home', so her information gathering was almost certainly unofficial.

'Do *you* think he'll pull it off?' I asked, seeing as how she seemed to know everything.

Mrs Moon pulled thoughtfully at a tangled skein of wool. 'I wouldn't like to say, not off the top of my head.'

Upstairs there was the sound of Dr Jefferies' raised voice and something crashing heavily on the floor. Mrs Moon looked up at the ceiling. 'But I think he's getting worried,' she said.

Shortly afterwards we heard the sound of feet clattering down the stairs and Dr Jefferies yelling, 'You're not responding. I put it down to being British. You don't want to succeed. Nobody in this country wants to succeed because if they're successful it'll mean they have to move their stiff little mouths and show a little enthusiasm.'

Mrs Moon and I worked our way to the crack in the kitchen door and peered through it. I had to crouch to find a place and had my nose pushed westwards by my fellow spy's large bosom.

We saw my mother clutching her black cardigan tightly round her, scuttling down the stairs followed by Dr Jefferies, who overtook her and blocked her way. He backed her into the corner of a landing halfway down the stairs. I could see that she was intent on finding a way past Dr Jefferies and stared at his corduroy trousers, first around them and then through them. How amazing, I thought, if she were to get down on all fours and crawl through his legs.

Dr Jefferies' face was grey. It was the colour of skin in a black and white photograph. He looked very tired and on edge as he leaned over my mother and shouted, 'This country has a cult of failure. They worship it. Only failures get any respect. How twisted can you get? They think that only failures have character. You have a Porsche, you're a nobody. Someone will scratch it. Or they'll take it away for a joyride. Everyone is so goddamn jealous they can't make a move.' He spat the words out with considerable anger. But the venom brought no colour to his face which remained the same lifeless shade of grey.

'And you,' he thrust his nose towards my mother like a swordsman putting home an épée. 'You're terrified to show any sign of improvement because you don't want to make anyone jealous.'

My mother edged round to the side of the landing but Dr

157

Jefferies shifted his position and continued to block her way. 'You work in a laundromat earning zilch so you get to be a card-carrying member of the suffering masses. No one can criticise you because you're the biggest failure on the block. That gets you kudos in this twisted country. That gives you worth, integrity. That gets you deified. And *you're* hooked on failure just like everyone else in this great British graveyard. Wake up! You've had the lessons. Show some sign of a change. Just because everyone else is sleep-walking you don't have to. Wake up for God's sake!'

Dr Jefferies had finished. He leaned back exhausted against the wall. I'd never seen him look so desperate. In fact, in some ways he was beginning to look like my mother. What a terrible fiasco it would be if he had unlearned his killer instinct!

I could see my mother, silent as usual, looking down the stairs at the Greek bust in the hallway with an almost nonchalant intensity. She bore the same expression as a chastised child who, out of pride, shows no remorse. Once again it seemed like progress to me. Before, my mother would have been destroyed by such a tirade.

But it was a very small sign. The big question was, how long would further progress take? Could Dr Jefferies continue to take the strain? Surely the forces of darkness in the shape of Eunice, Richard and Vincent would have won and demolished her before she had learned any useful killer instinct tricks. Was it all hopeless?

Mrs Cassels cast her eye over my interim report, and when I say cast her eye, I mean that. She was averse to reading long papers. Her state-school pupils, whom she remembered with such fondness, always wrote nice short papers on everything. 'They were concise,' she was always telling us by way of criticism of our long-winded efforts which took up a great deal of her marking time.

So she cast her eye over my paper when I delivered it to her, that is to say she flipped very quickly through the pages with her stubby, thick-knuckled fingers.

'I know that one of your relatives has been phoning our department but we have a long tradition of free thought and independent analysis at this school. We can't be censored.' She said it with a certain amount of disdain. Her old state school did not have traditions of any kind. They were too busy getting on with the hard realities of life. Traditions were for the fat-cat, fee-paying middle classes.

I could tell that what she actually meant was that Grandma Eunice's phone calls had really got up her nose. She read through one of my conclusions on the demanding nature of sex. 'I wouldn't say it's *that* compulsory,' she said.

'You're not out there on the front line, Mrs Cassels.'

She ignored that remark and flipped through a few more pages. 'Watch your spelling,' she said and threw my Sex 2000 survey across the desk. I picked it up gratefully and ran off before she changed her mind.

SEX 2000 – CONSUMER REPORT

How important, percentage wise, is sex in a marriage?

My father was in his pyjama bottoms and holding the Sunday paper protectively in front of him like a crucifix to ward off the evil demon daughter.

'Come in.' He looked surprisingly like our lodger on Sunday mornings: unshaven, hair uncombed, eyes unfocussed like Freddy's but much redder and more watery.

'You have the most beautiful flat,' I said appreciatively. I had not been to this one before and it was indeed beautiful. Big windows, balconies overlooking the Thames, two huge bathrooms with sunken baths and showers with not the smallest drop of sodium hyposulphate or a dangling wet film in sight. It was heaven.

'It's not mine. I can't afford a place like this,' he said quickly. 'I'm trying to sell it.'

'I really like sunken baths. Do they have whirlpools in them? Could I have a bath?'

My father stared at me, trying to focus. 'Jane, what the hell are you doing here?'

'Daddy,' I said. I was using this title to remind him of our relationship. 'I've come to ask you some questions for my school survey. It's very important to me. Before I had this survey I was listless and felt left out.'

'And how do you feel now?' he asked, as he groped for a cigarette in imaginary pockets around his bare chest and pyjama bottoms.

'I still feel listless and left out,' I replied. 'But I don't care about it any more because I have a goal in life. It's made all the difference to my mental health.'

He sighed, hurled his wad of newspapers at the coffee-table and sat down on one of his huge white sofas. My mother would have covered that sofa immediately with a blanket to stop it getting fingermarks.

'This is the sex survey that drove Frank to Australia?' he asked as he discovered a lone cigarette lying on the coffee-table. He put it in his mouth and left it there unlit while he concentrated on rubbing his fingers over his whiskery chin.

'Grandma Eunice just made that up. She's what drove him to Australia,' I said, sinking into the enveloping whiteness and softness of the sofa. The very softness of it was persuading me to give up my budding socialism. Wealth had its points.

'How long will this take?'

'Not long,' I said breezily.

I put my tape recorder on my lap and switched it on. 'I am speaking to Richard who sells houses and offices, and who plans to be a Member of Parliament if he can get selected. And elected, of course . . .'

I switched it off. 'I'll call you Richard so people won't know you're my father.'

My father's eyes were beginning to focus and therefore were growing more sinister. He stared at me, surprised at my presence, as if I had just fallen through a hole in the ceiling and landed on the sofa next to him. 'Jane, are you still doing this farcical sex survey?'

'Yes,' I said, exasperated. Why did adults never listen? Especially male adults. 'That's what we've been talking about since I walked in the door. We've *both* discussed it. How can you talk about something and not know you're doing it? Your mouth was going up and down, you were saying words, but . . .'

'All right, all right, all right,' he frowned and looked around the room as if trying to figure out where he was. 'You know it's very early, Jane.'

'It's half past eleven.'

He looked down at his naked chest, searching in the abundant dark hairs for confirmation of the late hour; finding none, he looked up unbelievingly at me.

'It's half past eleven,' I repeated.

'All right. Don't shout. You're not talking to your mother. Just because you bully her you can't do it to me.'

I switched on the tape recorder again. 'What part does sex play, percentage wise, in a marriage?'

My father stared at me, with the unlit cigarette still dangling from his mouth, and ran his fingers under the Sunday papers searching for a match. 'You know, Jane,' he

161

said, coughing. 'you seem to have forgotten somebody.'

'Who?'

'Frank.'

'Oh him.'

'Not "Oh him". You can't dismiss him like that. Frank is *very* important to all of us. And I repeat, *very* important. He's a millionaire. He owns a lot of land and a lot of property.' His hand alighted on a book of matches and he released it from under the newspapers. 'It would be immensely useful to me if I could make a few deals with him. It would be immensely useful to have a relative like that in our family. He has connections. He travels the world. He's a big fish.' He lit the cigarette and took a few energetic puffs, sucking like a baby with its first bottle. 'And you must not treat him lightly. He's not a joke. If *he* doesn't like sex surveys, *I* don't like sex surveys. And what's more, *you* don't like sex surveys. Men of his generation don't like to hear little girls talking about sex. You want to get out of that hovel in Shepherd's Bush don't you? You want to live in a place where you can invite your friends over? Then try to encourage Frank into our family, do what Grandma Eunice tells you and stop asking these bloody stupid questions.'

He leaned back and concentrated on his cigarette, giving it great love and attention, watching it so closely that he went a little cross-eyed as he put it in his mouth.

I was thinking furiously. Was there a way around this? But before I could say anything he went on. 'And I have to say this, Jane. If you continue with this, I will have to take you out of that school. I'm not going to pay an exorbitant amount of money to have you taught how to annoy Frank. They wouldn't let you do a sex survey at a comprehensive.'

There and then I discovered that I was a person who could make instant decisions. I surprised myself. It was a whole new element of my character that had not emerged before.

'All right Daddy,' I said meekly, 'I won't do it any more.'

My father looked astonished. He obviously had not expected it to be that easy. 'Good,' he said uncertainly. 'I'm glad you've come to your senses.'

'But,' I said, 'could you talk to me – just me – this isn't a survey. I'm going out with a boy next week. What do you do on a first date?'

'You don't do anything,' he said sharply. 'You're a child. You shouldn't be going out on a date.'

'But I'll have to get to know the opposite sex one of these days.'

My father's face contorted into a pugnacious, warlike mask, as he smashed the teeth of imaginary boyfriends. 'Better later than sooner. Boys are after only one thing.'

'Were you?'

'Er . . . well yes. I was a young man. I did what I was supposed to do.'

'And when you married Mummy, what happened?'

The mention of my mother deeply depressed my father. He sighed. 'Your mother. Your mother is different. She was nice enough to begin with.'

'Did sex play an important part in your marriage?' I asked.

He sighed again. 'Things were all right to begin with . . .'

'Are you talking about sex?'

'I suppose so, but your mother was so . . . so . . .'

'Sensitive?'

'Yes. I suppose that's it.'

'And that put you off so you looked for somebody who didn't put you off. Lots of people.'

My father writhed painfully on the sofa. 'I was driven to it. I didn't want to do that but it's very sad when two people get married and they don't suit each other. They're led into doing things that they hadn't planned.'

163

'So how important is sex in a perfect marriage, percentage wise?'

'Hundred per cent. It's important, Jane. It's the driving force. It's God's gift to mankind.'

'And that's why it's so sad that you married someone who only thought it was about twenty per cent important?'

'Twenty per cent? Is that what she told you?' My father was indignant.

'No, I'm really guessing. It's just that she doesn't go out looking for boyfriends.'

'Yes,' he nodded and flicked his ash into the saucer of a coffee-cup. 'Your mother is bloodless. She's always thinking. I've got nothing against thinking, but her thoughts don't lead to anything. She's a dead end.'

'She's learning the killer instinct.'

'With that idiot American? Only your mother would choose a quack like him. People in the United States live in a fantasy world, they have no concept of reality. The United States is full of these money grabbing psychologists peddling their third rate books. Your mother scraped the bottom of the barrel and pulled out the wormiest of the lot.'

'She's getting a little better. I heard her singing "We Shall Overcome" in the bathroom this morning.'

'Well whoopa dee doo dah. She can sing.'

I stayed for a while after that and made myself some lunch. My father said it was too early for him to eat. He had a disappointing selection in his refrigerator, so I had to cope with beans on toast and hot chocolate.

Later I wrote my conclusion. I had decided that as my father and Grandma Eunice did not like to hear about Sex 2000 I wouldn't tell them about it. I recorded my interview with my father by keeping my tape machine in my bag. The sound was muffled but adequate.

DELICATE MATTERS

Conclusion: Sex is a hundred per cent important in marriage. For some people this high percentage is too demanding on their time and energy. These people should probably not get married as they will get worn out.

CHAPTER
20

I met Garvie on Sunday afternoon at two-thirty outside Leicester Square tube station. He had wanted to meet me at seven-thirty on Saturday night like other normal human beings but my mother flipped about that. She said I had to come home in the daylight which was a *major* embarrassment. It was really uncool to have a date in the afternoon, but I could not figure out a way to get round it without having my mother trailing me the whole evening, ducking in and out of doorways, like a bumbling private detective.

As it was, I thought I caught sight of Freddy in his leather jacket dodging into McDonald's. Perhaps he had been talked into spying on us by my mother as she herself was stuck with a Sunday afternoon class on aggressive body language. But perhaps it wasn't Freddy. Could he be talked into anything by my mother?

Garvie was intent on finding the cinema and getting the tickets. He was deadly serious about it. He needed a goal as he didn't have anything to say if it wasn't about the tickets. So the date went like this: we went to the cinema, bought the tickets, went in, watched the film, walked to the tube station and said goodbye. That was it.

During the film he put his arm around my shoulders. This was very claustrophobic because once he'd got it there he didn't know how to get it back again. I bet he got pins and needles. I know my shoulders began to feel as if I were holding up the cinema roof. On this point I felt a little betrayed by all my Sex 2000 interviewees. Not one of them had mentioned possible muscle strain caused by dating. It was such a relief to stand up after the film and waggle my shoulders.

Freddy and my mother had done a great deal of conjecturing about what we would do after the film. Would we go to eat a hamburger? Would we go for a walk? I hadn't a clue about that and, unfortunately, neither had Garvie. I think it must have been his first date too. And the strain began to tell. We were both mightily relieved when we said goodbye at the tube station. I arrived home at four-fifty p.m. still in broad daylight, stiff and emotionally drained.

What had I learned about dating? (1) It was not nearly as pleasurable as everyone made it out to be. (2) It was, in fact, hard work. (3) Dating was both boring and stressful. And it was now clear to me why everyone drank so much alcohol when they went out on dates. It was to anaesthetise themselves so that they would not notice how difficult and tiresome dating could be.

The excursion however had served its purpose. I had now entered the ranks of those experienced women who had been out with a man. It made a considerable difference to the way I was perceived at school. Several girls from the élite group spoke to me on Monday morning when they heard that I'd 'been out'.

'Where did you go?' they wanted to know.

'Oh,' I said, thinking quickly. 'Well Garvie loves Italian food so we went to a little place in Soho.'

'Ooh!' They were impressed. 'And what's he like?'

'He's moody. Bouts of wild talking and then he gets very serious. He's quite a lot to handle.'

'Ooh. Did you go to a pub?'

'Of course. Garvie loves beer. But he doesn't get drunk easily. He can hold his liquor.'

'And what did you drink?'

What did I drink? What did I drink? 'Shandy. A couple of shandies.'

They were impressed. I had passed the test. I made a mental note to become more experienced at drinking alcohol. I knew nothing about it. I figured I had about a year before my ignorance would really show. A lot of the girls in the class above mine boasted about getting drunk on a regular basis and all their social engagements centred around the pub. If I didn't learn to be a good drinker I wouldn't have any friends.

'Is he a good kisser?' they asked.

'Fabulous,' I said.

'How far did he go?'

How far did he go? How far did he go? 'Um – well – he's really wild. I had to hold him back. We were right there in the middle of Leicester Square.'

'Ooh,' they all said.

I was a hit.

Things were getting pretty bad on the killer instinct front. My mother was beginning to have a mad, dazed look in her eye. I think it would have happened to anyone who had had as many lessons as she had. The constant running, martial arts, punch-bag boxing, and the assault courses would have been enough to exhaust anyone, but she also had the 'psychological' classes, plus her full-time work for Vincent. In the first few weeks she came home and described in detail everything Dr Jefferies had done but eventually, after a couple of months, she stopped talking about the classes and had, as I mentioned before, that mad, dazed look.

Mrs Moon was informative. 'He's teaching her to detach people from their actions now,' she told me one evening when I was hanging around her kitchen waiting for my mother. 'He's been working on that for weeks. He's telling her, when somebody puts her down she has to identify the behaviour. When she's got the behaviour all sorted out in her mind she won't be so scared of the person.'

'How do you mean?'

'She detaches it, you see. Then she has to ask where the behaviour is coming from. Why are they being aggressive? That sort of thing. It's not a person. It's behaviour.'

'Does that work?'

'Don't ask me.'

My mother looked more and more strange. Freddy said it was simply the look of someone who was overworked. But I felt it was more than that. She looked as if she were about to burst.

'Are you all right?' I asked her one night when she staggered in looking almost drunk from too much killer instinct.

'What's all right?' she asked and she threw her arms into the air like an actress playing Medea. 'Who knows what all right is?'

'How are your karate lessons coming along? Could you hurl Vincent over your shoulder?' I asked hopefully.

'Karate is kicking. Judo is more for throwing someone over your shoulder.' My mother made one of those 'Haaah' karate noises and jumped into what I suppose was an aggressive pose. And then she went into the kitchen and whistled, 'I'm a Yankee Doodle Dandy'. She'd never done that before.

'Is that the killer instinct?' I asked.

'What?'

'What you're doing.'

169

My mother threw her arms in the air again and put a carving knife between her teeth. 'If I get the killer instinct, there's only one person I want to kill.'

'Who's that?'

'Dr Arnold Jefferies.'

A few days later Grandma Eunice and Richard trailed my mother through the silent back streets of Holland Park to Dr Jefferies' house. It was the nearest thing to a high-speed chase you could expect from a car pursuing my mother in her rattling Hillman Imp; that is to say, it was a sedate chase. However when my mother caught sight of my father's shiny BMW in her rear-view mirror, she did try to shake them off.

Her idea of shaking them off was to drive around a small block six times until my father was mouthing unreadable swear words and Grandma Eunice was tapping the window signalling her to stop. But she didn't. She finally scooted to a halt outside Dr Jefferies' house and ran inside without pausing to lock her car door. (She had been hoping for a long time that someone would steal her car so she could get a better one with the insurance money, but so far no one had obliged her.)

I was not a witness to the scene that took place next but I've listened to all the accounts and I think I can safely say it went like this:-

My mother was going up the stairs for another class in aggressive role-playing, when the door-bell rang and Mrs Moon went to open the door. As soon as the door was opened my father and Eunice pushed their way into the hall and stood by the Greek bust yelling, 'Louise! Come here.'

Dr Jefferies heard the noise and came out on to the landing, leaned over the bannister and said, 'What the hell are they doing here?'

170

My mother, stuck halfway up the stairs as usual, said, 'It's my mother and ex-husband.'

'Oh,' said he, extremely intrigued. 'It's *them*.'

And he went down the stairs and looked them over with great curiosity, as if they were two challenging rats just delivered to his laboratory.

'What,' said Grandma Eunice in her most strident voice, 'are you doing with my daughter?'

'I'm teaching her the killer instinct,' he said, dead pan, his hands in his pockets. Mrs Moon, standing by the kitchen door, watched fascinated.

Richard was instantly belligerent. 'You're not teaching her anything. You're using her to sell your book. It's another example of sleazy American exploitation. We're sick of your types coming into this country, bringing down the standards. You're not concerned with her welfare at all.'

Dr Jefferies leaned against a bookcase and kept his hands in his pockets, casual American style, and replied, 'I suppose *you* are.'

'Yes,' said Richard getting a little red in the face, 'I am concerned with my wife's welfare. She's a very sensitive, fragile personality and she can't handle money grubbing exploiters like you. She needs protection. We've come to take her away.'

'Yes,' said Grandma Eunice, 'we want her back. This ridiculous brain-washing must stop. She just can't cope with all this rubbish. She may never recover. She's always been very imaginative. She has to be around a positive influence.'

'Ho ho ho,' said Dr Jefferies like Santa Claus. 'I like that. It's Francis of Assisi and Florence Nightingale come to take her into their protective care. What do you say to that, Louise?' And he stood back like someone setting his pitbull on to intruders and waited for my mother to do her stuff.

My mother stuck to her corner on the stairs and surveyed

the situation thoughtfully but did nothing.

'Go on,' said Dr Jefferies. 'We went over this yesterday. You know exactly what to do.'

But my mother did nothing.

Grandma Eunice was getting impatient. 'Louise, we can't wait here all night.'

'Louise!' said Richard.

'Louise!' said Dr Jefferies.

Then Richard pushed past Dr Jefferies and ran up the stairs, grabbed my mother's wrist and pulled her down the stairs.

When Richard reached the last step, Dr Jefferies caught hold of his arm and loosened his grip on my mother's wrist and a scuffle ensued, with my mother like a rabbit between two snarling, hungry hyenas.

'Let go of her,' shouted Richard, his face getting extremely red. 'Go back to the slimy cesspools in your own country and get some stupid American to work on. Don't take a decent woman like Louise.'

'Don't fight,' screamed Eunice. 'You're hurting my daughter.'

'What did I tell you, Louise, do you remember the self-delusion lessons? They want to screw you and be made into saints for it. It's a classic British delusion,' shouted Dr Jefferies, always the teacher, as he tugged so hard at Richard's arm that the jacket of his Valentino suit came off.

My mother, who so far had not said a word, suddenly did a funny little movement. 'It was karate,' Mrs Moon told me afterwards. 'It was not karate,' said my mother, 'I just wriggled a bit and got away.'

Whether or not it was a killer instinct movement, my mother certainly escaped from their clutches, ran out of the front door and drove away to an undisclosed destination. She did not go home immediately because she knew Richard

172

and Eunice would look for her there.

They came storming into our flat, my father with his jacket slightly torn and his tie undone and Grandma Eunice, wide-eyed with the horror of it all. 'Where's your mother?' they asked, leaning across the chest of drawers in the doorway of our heavily over-furnished bedroom.

I was sitting on the bed, listening to Capital Radio and doing my geometry homework.

'She's at Dr Jefferies,' I said.

'Oh no she's not,' said Grandma Eunice. 'She's given us the slip.'

'No kidding,' I said.

They didn't like that. No kidding was the sort of thing Americans said. Richard went into the living room and examined his wounds while Eunice looked through the kitchen drawers and cupboards making 'tch tch' noises of disapproval. She had not been inside our humble flat for several years and was checking to see if our standards had improved.

My father patted a scratch on his face and said, 'We're going now. Where's the lodger?'

'He's in his dark room. He can't come out.'

'He's still here?' asked Eunice. She and my father exchanged serious glances. 'Your mother,' said Eunice, 'is out of control. She's being poisoned by the American. She mustn't go near him again.'

'Tell her to phone me when she gets in,' said Richard.

'It's vital,' said Eunice. 'Frank's coming back. He'll be here in two weeks. We must have things sorted out by then.'

'Remember this, Jane. Die before you marry an American.'

They left. Dr Jefferies phoned and asked where my mother was and I had to tell him she was nowhere to be found. An hour later she walked in with that mad, dazed expression on her face.

'Where have you been?' I asked, 'Everyone's been looking for you.'

'Yes,' she said. 'I'm a prize piece of meat.' She leaned against the door frame, once again in that rather theatrical way she'd had of doing things lately.

'What are you going to do?' I asked, very worried. 'And don't say you're going to commit suicide.'

'I thought I'd watch television. I haven't had a night off in ages.'

She still looked slightly weird, slightly mad, so I said, 'What a good idea. It's a good idea to have a change. And it'll help all the killer instinct instruction jell.'

'Jell?' she said bitterly, 'jell? Killer instincts don't jell.'

And she sat down and watched a documentary on female circumcision, not exactly a cheerful subject, but it seemed to distract her for a brief moment.

I was grateful for that.

SEX 2000 – CONSUMER REPORT

Is the sexual instinct like the killer instinct? Can it be taught?

The morning after the fight between Richard and Dr Jefferies, my mother was out very early, jogging around Hyde Park, and then after work she had her usual Tuesday night 'attack and kill' punch-bag class. She was back on schedule.

Even so, it was unnerving to have her return home again with that strange expression on her face. I didn't know what to do about it. The best idea I could come up with was to go to Dr Jefferies' house after school on Thursday and ask if I could interview him for Sex 2000. If he agreed, and it was a big if, I thought it might offer me an opportunity to express my concerns about my mother at the same time.

I had to wait for half an hour because Dr Jefferies was out.
When he came in carrying a heavy briefcase and wearing
one of those pale raincoats that Americans wear in London,
he seemed distracted but he *agreed* to talk to me. What a
surprise. I think the big confrontation with Richard and
Grandma Eunice may have softened him up a bit.

And he was the first adult to be unconcerned about the
subject matter. 'You want to ask me about sex?' he asked as
if he were talking about the weather. The only thing that
worried him was that I would overlap my mother's evening
session, which was due to start at six-thirty.

Mrs Moon's ears were flapping in the kitchen doorway as
he led me along a dark corridor, wallpapered floor to ceiling
with books on philosophy and psychology, to the small
study on the ground floor. It was the same room, not far
from the kitchen, to which Mrs Moon had taken my mother
on that first fatal visit when she collapsed in floods of tears.

'I won't take you to the study upstairs. Mrs Moon won't
have to pretend to clean the stairs if we stay down here.' Dr
Jefferies threw his raincoat over a chair and then with a
sadistic gleam in his eye he said, 'I'm using her for a paper
on acute nosiness in post-menopausal women.'

This remark was not made for my benefit. In reply there
was the sound of a saucepan banging angrily in the kitchen.
It seemed that master and servant communicated by dropping heavy objects.

Two minutes later Mrs Moon's large self loomed in the
doorway bearing a plate piled high with ginger biscuits and
processed cheese wedges in silver paper. 'I expect the child
will be hungry,' she said vengefully and slapped the plate
down on a small leather footstool which was close to my
chair. Then she stamped out.

Dr Jefferies eyed the plate jealously for a few seconds

before crossing the room and taking a huge handful of biscuits and cheese wedges. Realising that he might do the same again and clean the plate before I'd had a go, I also took a huge handful and placed them on my lap.

During the interview, both Dr Jefferies and I were much occupied with finding the little red tag which, when pulled with care, neatly removed the silver paper from the soft wedge of cheese.

'What do you want to know?' asked Dr Jefferies, peeling the cheese and stuffing it into his mouth along with one of the biscuits he had lined up along his thigh. I could tell by the way he chewed one biscuit and followed it thoughtlessly with another that he was not a gourmet of any kind. He showed no loving care for a good ginger biscuit but just ate it. What a waste of a biscuit, I thought.

'Can you use the killer instinct in sex?' I was hoping this would be the sort of question he would take to.

But a small sneer of disapproval came over his face. '*In* sex? Do you mean for sexual conquests?'

I had thrown the question together and was not quite sure, but I said, 'Yes.'

He looked at me as if I were a really small squirt. 'Why don't you ask me if the sexual instinct is like the killer instinct? Ask me if it's not really an instinct but something we learn. That's a more interesting question.'

'All right. Is the sexual instinct like the killer instinct?'

A light immediately came into his eyes. 'As far as I'm concerned, yes. It's not a view that everyone holds.'

I was glad things were running smoothly now. 'Why isn't it a view that everyone holds?'

'Because everyone likes to think that they're a sitting duck and that sex hits them. It's a convenient belief. It lets everyone off the hook. But it's quite unscientific.'

I thought it was too early to squeeze in a question about

my mother so I asked instead, 'How do you mean, it lets them off the hook?'

'I mean that sex relies largely upon the imagination and most people have extremely lazy imaginations. They get spoon-fed sexual fantasies from one generation to the next, from one century to another.' He munched thoughtfully. 'They are puppets dangling on the strings of sexual history. That sounds quite poetic doesn't it?' He looked pleased with himself. It was extremely rare for him to look like that.

But I was confused by the metaphors. 'You said people aren't sitting ducks but they are puppets.' I didn't mean to be annoying, but it was immediately obvious that I was.

He did not like being challenged and scowled. 'I'm saying that they're not sitting ducks, and neither are they puppets. They *think* they're puppets.'

'But they're not?'

'No.'

There was a pause. I counted that I had eight ginger biscuits and four cheese wedges on my lap. And he had six biscuits left, after eating several, plus three cheese wedges. There were three biscuits and no cheese left on the plate on the leather footstool.

Dr Jefferies spoke once more. 'Sex is mythology. Everything to do with sex – romance, passion, eroticism – they're all mythology, even pleasure. Now that's a difficult one because pleasure is pleasure, right?'

'Right,' I said. Who was I to disagree?

'But what you actually get in sex is a building up of tension and then a release. Like a bowel movement. The two are very similar except a bowel movement doesn't have the weight of mythology around it. And of course, if you don't have a bowel movement you die. Whereas you can live without sex. Mythology says you can't but you can.'

I could not understand how he could eat and talk about

bowel movements at the same time. But he went on regardless. 'Sexual tension is caused by myth, legend. We all respond like automatons and then we need release. Like Pavlov's dog.'

'Is that a bad thing?'

Dr Jefferies crunched noisily on another biscuit. The crunching sound filled the room. 'Sex has a built-in problem. Two people like each other. You bring sex into the equation and immediately there's distrust. How much do you like me? How much do you like me for sex? Which comes first? It sets up a division. Civil war of the human race.'

'Oh,' I said and tried to unwrap a cheese wedge in a thoughtful, academic way. In those days my mind began to wander if anyone harped on one point too much but I didn't want him to notice.

'You get jealousy,' he went on. 'You get hatred. I'd say most people would be better off without sex. But there's a pressure to perform.'

Now he had my attention. 'Oh I know! I only have till the end of next year. I know that sounds like a long time but most of my friends are way ahead of me and if I haven't done it by then I'll be an outcast.'

'Done it by then?' He looked mystified.

I backtracked. 'Well you can actually get away with it until you've done your GCSEs. But you are *getting away with it*. It's not a preferred option. After that, if you're still a novice, you are considered a total noodle.'

'Oh,' he said. It was obvious that I had disturbed his train of thought with my petty problems. But he said quickly, as if to get it over and done with because it was boring, 'Should we discourage our children from early sexual experience? Yes I think so. It's a short cut. They miss the scenic route. They miss some basic steps of learning about our fellow beings that only come through the many stages of friendship. You probably don't agree but you've been mesmerised by all the hype just like everyone else.'

'Yes,' I said. I certainly didn't want to be different.

'Children have to learn that sex is always a trade off. Early sex is a lower contemplation of the mind involving thoughts about the body. These offer limited scope to the mind of a child who has infinite capacities and should not be confined in this way.' He peered through his glasses to see if that was enough to satisfy me then he got back on track. 'The question you should probably ask me now is, could I teach anyone to conquer the so-called sexual instinct?'

Dutifully I asked, 'Could you teach anyone to conquer the so-called sexual instinct?'

He put his hands, clasped together, on his head, gazed up at a spider on the ceiling and considered the question thoughtfully. 'Yes I think I could.'

'How would you do it?'

'Well,' he said, 'if, say, you were a person who was a slave to sex, I'd begin by examining any firm convictions you had about sex. For instance, the idea that sex is shocking should be removed first of all. It's the so-called shocking element that makes it so compulsive. And of course it causes social embarrassment, blackmail, disclosure in the tabloid newspapers, personal ruin.'

'Would that be difficult, to stop someone thinking it's shocking?'

'Yes. And you know why? Vested interests. There's a great big machinery out there keeping sex shocking. It's still the quickest and easiest way to make money, sell something or ruin anybody.'

The sound of Mrs Moon singing 'When Irish Eyes Are Smiling' wafted in from the kitchen and we both paused to listen to her wobbling, cracked voice.

Dr Jefferies grimaced and then went on, 'It's difficult to

make anyone change their attitudes because they think that everything to do with sex is carved in stone. And they think their sexual self is their identity.'

'Isn't it?'

'Absolutely not.' He chewed on a biscuit. 'The sexual is a minuscule part of the human identity. But as I said, you have the heavy mythology and the tremendous hype that goes with all matters sexual. Hypnotism. Sex is hypnotism. People have to wake up out of the long dream. Sex is deadly confinement. Small thinking. You have to unhypnotise people. Then they'd open up their thinking to vast vistas of opportunity. The universe would change.'

He looked inspired by the idea but I thought it was time to confront him with my real reason for being there.

Before I could get a word out, he went on. 'Of course you also have to ask yourself, what would happen to sex if you removed the guilty excitement and the violence, imagined and real. Would sexual arousal become difficult?' He looked at me as if I had the answer. I shrugged. How should I know? My afternoon at the cinema with Garvie had left me, as far as experience was concerned, a little on the limited side.

He had to answer himself. 'No,' he said firmly. 'Sexual arousal would not be difficult because the imagination which drives sex is infinitely adaptable. It does not drive us. We drive it.'

I couldn't wait any longer. 'Do you think my mother's all right?'

He looked surprised. I'd disturbed his train of thought again. He blinked and tried to focus on the question. He stared at all the books piled in heaps around the floor, books with long titles, many of them in foreign languages, particularly German. Once he'd focussed he gave me a beady look. 'You think it's not working. You think I'm out of my mind. You think your mother is the same as she always was.'

'No I don't. She's different. I can see she's different.'

'How is she different?'

'She's got a mad look in her eye.'

'And she says she wants to kill me?'

My jaw fell. 'How did you guess?'

'Aha!' He waved his fist triumphantly. 'I thought she did!'

I felt awful. I'd given my mother away. But I had to find out. 'Will the mad look go away? Will she get better? Is she the very first human you've tried it on? When you worked on rats did they get a mad look?'

He looked offended by the question. 'Rats don't have expressions like human beings.'

'Do they go mad?'

'They can act in ways that appear mad.'

'Oh.' I felt very despondent.

Dr Jefferies made an effort to cheer me up. 'I would say that the so-called mad look in your mother's eye is a positive sign.'

'It's not a mental breakdown?'

'I can't promise that. The human psyche is complex. It reacts to pressure in a thousand different ways.'

My heart sank.

Dr Jefferies picked up his last biscuit and chewed it compassionately. 'Don't look so down. Your mother has a constitution stronger than any sewer rat I've ever met.'

He meant it as a compliment.

I stayed long enough to clean up the last three biscuits on the plate and then I left. I got away just before my mother arrived for the evening session.

Conclusion: It is possible that the human race has been hypnotised for thousands of years into believing there is such a thing as sexual instinct. If this is true, the first person to snap out of it will feel very peculiar.

CHAPTER

21

I battled my way through the entwined cables and golf equipment to Freddy's room. 'Did you know,' I announced, 'that the sexual instinct isn't an instinct? We learn it. By a sort of hypnotic process.'

There was not much to be seen of Freddy, apart from chemical stains of varying hues spattered across the back of his metallic grey T-shirt. He was bent over his desk, rifling through the drawers, muttering irritably, 'Bloody hell ... bloody hell.'

I sat down on his now not so new navy-blue Ralph Lauren sheets. 'What do you think? I'd like some feedback.'

Freddy turned and hissed accusingly, 'I'm missing Tipp-Ex, PrittStick and scissors.'

'Oh ...'

'Yes?'

'I think I may have borrowed them.'

'You think? Did you or didn't you?'

'I suppose I did. Yes I did.'

The dark stubble on Freddy's chin bristled in agitation. 'You little turd. I've told you before. They do *not* leave my room. I'm using them for my work *all* the time. Get your own bloody PrittStick.'

He rampaged out of his room and made an assault on my

room, leaping from one piece of furniture to another like an experienced mountain rescuer, as he searched for my pencil-case. Items often fell between the stocked boxes and chest of drawers in my room and disappeared forever into inaccessible fissures and caverns, but Freddy managed to come up with three old pencil-cases before he found my current one. Unfortunately it did not contain any PrittStick or Tipp-Ex.

'I'm sorry, Freddy, I had some of my own but it'd all dried up. PrittStick is so useful. It's hard to get through the day without it.'

'I don't want a bloody commercial, I want the PrittStick.' Freddy became a glowering monster, filling my room with dark clouds of wrath.

'It might be at school.'

'If it is at school, I'll wring your neck. How many times do I have to tell you my room is not a treasure trove for you to dip your snotty little nose into?'

'I realise you're upset Freddy—'

'Upset? I'm frenzied. I'm about to rip your arms off one at a time and throw them out of the window to a passing dog.'

'Just over PrittStick?'

'YES! Over PrittStick! I need it NOW and it's not here. AND I need the Tipp-Ex and my good scissors. If you're going to rip off my scissors why don't you take the crappy ones?'

At that moment the phone rang. The nearest phone was on the white wicker nightstand by the window, that is to say, right where I was sitting.

'Get that,' ordered Freddy. It was after office hours so he was not too concerned about it being his agent.

I put on my most conciliatory and humble face. 'Please, Freddy. You get it. It's Garvie.'

'Then you get it.'

'I don't want to speak to him.'

183

'Why not?'

'Because I can't. Please, please, Freddy. Don't make me talk to him.'

The phone continued to ring. Freddy was standing on an antique sideboard with his legs astride and his arms folded, rather like a resentful genie who'd just popped unwillingly out of a lamp.

'You're getting like your mother. Answer the bloody phone! Don't start acting like her.'

'Please, please, Freddy. It's just so hard. I can't.'

It was impossible for me to convey to Freddy the dark horror I had been feeling about Garvie's phone calls. I felt so sickeningly trapped by them. They were sentences of death. I had even stopped eating chocolate, they made me so nervous. He had phoned five times since our date. He was actually quite capable of maintaining something like a conversation on the phone (as opposed to face to face, when he clammed up). So the conversation, painful though it was, was not the major part of the problem. What terrified me were his vague mumblings about meeting again. I could not face it. What on earth would be expected of me on a *second* date? And that was not all, there was also the fact that his happiness and status now depended upon me, what I said, how I responded. It was far too much for me to bear. I wanted to run a hundred miles and hide.

'Answer the bloody phone!'

'No.'

Freddy, looking like thunder, jumped across the bed and grabbed the phone.

'Yes!' he spat out furiously.

It was Garvie.

'I'm afraid she's gone out to buy some PrittStick,' said Freddy. 'No, I don't know when she'll be back.' He threw the receiver in the direction of the phone. I caught it before it went through the window. 'Next time *you* answer it and you put that kid out of his misery.' Freddy clambered over two packing cases and a desk towards the doorway. 'I can't cope with two spineless women in this flat. You speak to him and if you don't want to see him, say so. Don't act like your dumb, gutless mother.'

'I don't like to think that I'll break his heart if I say I don't want to see him anymore. It's an awesome responsibility,' I said, crawling over the furniture in pursuit. 'It was much easier when I had a crush on him. Now it's a duty.'

'That's life, Jane. Face up to it. You have to learn that every time you make a move it screws up somebody. Life is a very messy business.'

I groaned. 'Why does it have to be like that?'

'Don't ask me. Just be a man and put up with it.'

I followed Freddy across the living-room towards his room. He turned when he got to his door. 'I suppose you think you can come in and rip off some more of my stuff?'

'No honestly, Freddy. I'm racking my brains to think if maybe your PrittStick *isn't* at school. Maybe it's in my make-up case. And if it's not, I'll get you some. I promise.'

I found the stolen articles entangled in the duvet on my bed, the place where I did all my homework. I returned them to a sullenly grateful Freddy and then returned to the prospect of further calls from Garvie.

I couldn't think of what to say so I took the phone off the hook for the sake of a peaceful evening. Two days later I faced up to my duty and talked to Garvie.

'Hello, Garvie. I'd love to see you but I'm studying for exams. That takes up all the time I have off at the weekend. Then there's the summer holidays when I'll be on holiday. Then after that there's the play rehearsal in the autumn term, and then it's Christmas and Christmas is going to be really frantic. It's going to be a really busy year. I'm really sorry. The year's completely taken up.'

I heard from Andy that Garvie went round his school telling everyone that his girlfriend had dumped him. I felt very bad about it. He stopped working for Vincent so I didn't see him any more. And the worst thing about it was I really liked Garvie.

But the good news was that I had gone out on a date, had an emotional relationship and broken it off successfully. That was a major accomplishment. I was an experienced, world-weary woman who could talk about her unhappy love affair, and the problems of handling men. I had made enormous progress.

A week after that, I wheedled my way into getting an invitation from Sophia to go to a pub in Chiswick. From an ethical point of view she was not in a position to invite me, as she was planning to gatecrash another group's party. This party, or rather an evening in a pub, had been set up by three 'almost elité' girls who were famous for their hard-to-prove, lurid tales of pub life, in which they got off with much older men or were the centre of a fracas caused by their presence.

'You can come, if you like,' said Sophia. 'But we don't want a big crowd. They'll ask for ID if there's too many of us.'

'They won't guess we're thirteen?'

'Two of us are fourteen,' she said snidely. 'Just look confident. And bored. They'll never guess.'

I practised looking bored in the mirror. I tried it with earrings, without earrings, with and without lipstick, hair up and down, with hat, without hat. The more I looked and manipulated, the younger I became. What was it that made me look so young? It was the size of my face. It wasn't big enough. The lips, the nose, the cheeks, the skull on top of it, were all miniaturised. They had not enlarged into a full-fleshed, big-nosed adult face. I needed a bigger face.

When my mother came in from her 'absolute power' class, I told her I would be going to the pub on Friday.

That mad look that my mother brought home from Dr Jefferies' classes was developing into a slightly out of focus, frazzled expression. She turned this hazy, fuzzy beam on me and said, 'You're not going.'

'What do you mean?' I asked. 'Everyone's going.'

'Not to a pub.'

I sighed patronisingly. 'Not to a pub? It's what girls do now. Everyone hangs out at the pub.'

'Well you're not. Thirteen is too young to hang around pubs.'

'Oh God, you're so old-fashioned. It's not 1066 anymore. Young people go to pubs. It's what they do.'

My mother examined herself in the mirror over the fireplace, the same chipped gilt-framed mirror I had been using to inspect any signs of adulthood; she leaned towards the glass and rearranged her face so that it was better looking. 'Is that a dictionary definition?' she asked, lifting her eyebrows and chin. 'Young person. Someone who goes to pubs? Let me tell you, we're starting a new dictionary. Young person. Definition. Someone who realises that they're young.'

I scowled at her mask-like reflection. 'Do you realise that you'll be the only mother who won't let her daughter go out on Friday?'

'I don't care what other mothers do. I care what I do. Other mothers can drop their children into the depths of depravity, opium dens, brothels. That's their business. It's not mine.' My mother turned from the mirror with an authoritative sweep and went, with some grandeur, into the kitchen.

Oh hell! This was a worst case scenario played out before

my eyes. She was using her killer instinct on me. The one who'd encouraged her to learn it. What if I were the only one she would ever be able to use it on? What if that one small piece of killer instinct that she had imbibed was turned forever and only on me and no one else? What a disaster.

SEX 2000 – FOUR CONSUMER REPORTS

(1) How valuable is sex? Are you only valuable when you're sexually attractive?

Grandma Eunice said, 'It's terrible being an old woman. Have you seen the way people look at old ladies in the street?'

'How do they look?'

'Right through them. Already I'm a ghost. When I was young and beautiful everyone looked at me. I couldn't go anywhere without turning heads. Now I don't exist.'

I mentioned this to Sophia during our geography class and she replied, 'When I'm an old woman I'll insist that people look at me.'

I said, 'Why do you want to be looked at? I don't want anyone to look at me. It makes me really self-conscious and paranoid. I want to walk along the street and be a free woman.'

'Then take your granny with you when you go out, Jane.'

Conclusion: In order for women to be free they have to be ugly and old. Some women find this too high a price to pay for freedom.

(2) Is sex not as important as everyone says?

'Did you know,' I told Freddy, as he lifted a wet film out of our yellowing bath, 'that ten per cent of all executives think golf is more important than sex?'

'Well whaddyaknow,' said Freddy.

'Do you think that indicates that sex is not so important as everyone says?'

'No,' he said, as he clipped the film on to a washing line to dry. 'Look at it another way. That statistic means that ninety per cent of all executives think sex is more important than golf.'

Conclusion: Golf can make people lose interest in sex. However, as golf courses take up so much room and not everyone can afford golf clubs, it will not have a great effect on sex as a whole.

(3) Are men smarter than women?

I asked Dolores about this matter as she seemed to be knowledgeable on the subject of men. She was vacuuming the leopard-skin seat covers in her Mini Metro.

'No,' she said, switching off the vacuum cleaner. The tiny gold-painted flowers on her nails glinted in the sunlight. 'Men think they're smarter because women tell them they are. But every woman knows she's smarter than the man she's with, and more thoughtful.'

'Why do women keep quiet about it?'

'Because men get very upset when they find out. But women should be running the world. We wouldn't have wars if women were in charge.'

I nodded in agreement. It was never a good idea to disagree with Dolores.

'Men hate women,' she said. 'That's why they make all the movies about mutilating women. It turns them on. If you loved dogs would your idea of a good night out be going to a dog torturing movie? You'd only enjoy it if you hated dogs, right? The same goes for women. Men hate them.'

'Some women go to those movies too,' I ventured.

'Then they're a traitor to their sex,' Dolores snapped.

Conclusion: Women have to pretend that they are stupid when they are with men so that men don't get nervous. Although some women may find this difficult to do, others will find it incredibly easy.

(4) What is better than sex?

What the customers in Vincent's Launderette replied to this question:

'I like toast and marmalade better than sex.'

'I like Elvis singing "Are You Lonesome Tonight?" better than sex.'

'Nothing is better than sex.'

'I like my kids saying, Mum I love you, better than sex.'

'I like walking along the Uxbridge Road on a Sunday morning better than sex.'

'Sex is overrated.'

'Sex is dead.'

'Sex keeps you young.'

'Sex makes you old. I've had eleven kids, all on account of sex. Before I started I had a twenty-two inch waist. Now look at me.'

'Sex makes the world go round.'

'I like Bingo better than sex.'

'I like having my feet massaged better than sex.'

'Here. You've got a cheek asking me that. It's none of your bloody business.'

Conclusion: It is possible that taking your clothes to the launderette causes loss of interest in sex.

CHAPTER
22

Grandma Eunice and Aunt Joanna arrived in a taxi. They descended the stairs into our basement flat, like two queen bats dropping into hell. Aunt Joanna, with her hair scraped back and bright neon lips, carried a Gucci garment bag through the front door and pushed it into my arms.

'Hold that, darling,' she said to me and, having freed herself, dusted her hands against each other, seemingly removing any soiling that may have been caused by walking through the door.

Grandma Eunice, well-corseted in a black, ambassadorial dress and lots of rattling gold jewellery, swung through the door, stood with her legs astride, and said, 'Where's your mother?'

'She's getting ready,' I said.

Getting ready was obviously a crime. 'I *thought* she would,' Eunice muttered accusingly.

'Isn't she supposed to?' I asked.

'Not if she's going to put on that hoeing get-up. I expect she's dragging it out of a bin-bag right now.' She turned her attention to me, eyeing every item of my clothing with growing concern; by the time she reached my Doc Martens a deep frown crossed her well-powdered face. '*Don't* think you're going to wear that.'

'I'm not ready yet. These are my old jeans.'

'Is that what they are?' Eunice sniffed and looked around the living-room. 'Louise!'

Aunt Joanna prowled towards the bedroom, opened the door, and was brought to a halt by the solid wall of furniture which filled the room. Peering around a polished walnut chest of drawers she caught my mother standing on the bed holding an ankle-length patchwork skirt to her waist.

'Oh!' said my mother, jumping guiltily. 'Joanna! What are you doing here?'

Joanna looked at the patchwork skirt clutched in my mother's hands. 'What's that? An old curtain?'

Eunice burst in after her and was also stopped abruptly by the log jam of furniture. 'Louise. How can you live in this jumble, this storage locker?' She spied the skirt, which my mother was now half hiding behind her back. 'Oh no! Put that away. Joanna's brought something for you. Let Joanna take over.'

Joanna looked around at the imbroglio of desks, chests and boxes in dismay. 'How am I supposed to do anything in here? There's nowhere to stand.'

'You can stand on the bed,' I said, stating the obvious. My mother was still on the bed. Her stance, though, was now leaning towards cowering as her shoulders slumped and her knees buckled. It was discouraging to see her revert to type so quickly.

It was six-thirty. At eight o'clock we were all expected at my father's flat in Chelsea Harbour where he was giving a welcome home family dinner for Frank, the wandering millionaire returned from Australia. The dinner was to be catered by some fancy cordon bleu cooks, which I was most grateful for. My father certainly could not have cooked the dinner himself. His one and only dish was eggs and bacon, which he made by burning the bacon first, then scrambling the eggs in the burnt bacon pan and producing black-flecked eggs.

Because I was looking forward to a French dinner, cooked by experts, I put up with being dressed by Aunt Joanna. For my evening ensemble she produced from her garment bag a pale olive-green baggy silk dress. It was meant to be baggy and gathered together with a thin cream belt. However it lost most of its bagginess on me, so Joanna covered it with a cream linen jacket. I thought I looked like a bowel of pistachio and vanilla ice-cream.

My mother meekly submitted to being dressed in a navy-blue velvet suit with pearls and matching shoes that were too big and had to be stuffed with tissue. Joanna produced curling tongs, mousse and sprays, and set about our hair. My mother's hair required a deluge of spraying and curling but I was discovered to be 'unwashed'. My clothes were pulled off and my head was pushed over the bath while Joanna attacked me with shampoo and a hand shower. Then she dried, combed and set my hair solid like a crash helmet so that not one hair could fall out of place and ruin the honour of our united family.

We trooped out like captured natives dressed in conquerors' clothes and were driven, submissive and unprotesting, to the victory dinner in Aunt Joanna's car. For it was a victory that Frank had agreed to come. Hopes had been rekindled that Grandma Eunice might catch him yet.

'Thank God we caught you in time,' said Eunice as we stopped and started along the congested Earl's Court Road. 'What a fiasco if you'd worn that patchwork quilt, Louise. You'll have to stop wearing home furnishings. It speaks volumes.'

'And thank God I could do the hair and the make-up,' said Aunt Joanna, 'there's no hair spray or mousse anywhere in that flat. I've never known anything like it. She was going to walk in with her hair hanging round her ears like an old dish mop. And Jane hadn't even washed her hair!'

'She doesn't like water,' said my mother miserably.

'She'll have to learn to like it. She can't go through life unwashed. No wonder she's unpopular.' Grandma Eunice rattled her shiny gold jewellery in disgust.

When we arrived at my father's front door we were met by a maid in uniform. She escorted us into the living-room which was set for action, surfaces cleared and polished, and every nook artfully spotlighted. My father was out on the terrace looking anguished amid a cloud of cigarette smoke. He came hurrying to meet us with the wind from the Thames billowing wispy net curtains behind him. 'Where were you? Frank's getting here any minute.'

'We've averted a disaster,' said Eunice. 'They can't be left to their own devices. We were a hair's breadth away from having a couple of bag ladies turn up here tonight. Joanna's done a miraculous overhaul on them.'

Joanna smiled modestly. 'It's amazing what designer clothes and a lot of mousse will do.'

My mother and I hung our heads humbly as we submitted ourselves to inspection by my father. He nodded approvingly. 'Yes. This is what I've been talking about. If they would look like this I could introduce them to a few people. They could help the situation.'

'How are your prospects for selection going?' asked Eunice.

'Not too brilliantly at the moment. I was hoping to bring Louise and Jane on to the scene months ago but Louise is never home. And even if she is she needs to be prepared, she can't be allowed to turn up willy nilly.'

Eunice glanced at Joanna. 'We can help, can't we, Joanna?' She leaned over to Richard and, in a whisper we could all hear, said, 'I see it's useless asking her to do anything. If you need her any time Joanna and I will go over and get her ready. Don't give her an option. She can't handle options. She has to be led.'

I escaped to look in the kitchen where an intense young woman in a mini-skirt was taking a dish of something rolled in pastry out of the oven. It smelled wonderful. 'What's that?' I asked, with supreme interest.

She mumbled something like, 'Gepatti Krott', which, I found out later, was game pâté en croûte.

Another intense young woman was throwing handfuls of crab meat, parsley, breadcrumbs and grated cheese into a bowl, mixing it very fast and then stuffing the mixture into chicken breasts. Her face was pink with exertion. I asked if she needed any help but she didn't answer.

It was quite obvious they wanted me to clear off but before I went I found out what was for pudding – a choice of lemon soufflé or raspberry tart. I was close to ecstatic.

When Frank arrived everybody wagged their tails furiously but he didn't seem to be put off by it. He was probably used to people going overboard when they met him. It was becoming clear to me that all millionaires lived a life of heavily wagged tails.

The eating of the dinner went very smoothly, without anyone saying anything too unfortunate. Grandma Eunice had said to me just before Frank arrived, 'Don't upset the apple cart, Jane.' And I thought I was a model of discretion. However, when the maid put a stuffed chicken breast in front of Frank, I was inspired to say, 'Did you know a farmyard animal is slaughtered every second in Britain?' I thought that was an interesting contribution but Eunice and Joanna gave me deadly serpent looks and I realised I'd said the wrong thing again.

But the food was mouthwateringly delicious, the conversation moved on and I was happy to keep silent after that and eat. Eating opportunities as good as this did not offer themselves every day of the week.

And Frank did not seem upset by my remark. In fact by the time we got to the pudding he was getting quite jolly and his sophisticated, mid-Atlantic accent was becoming more Birmingham. He even raised his glass and said, 'You're a wonderful family. The world may be falling apart but we still have hope if there are families like this.'

After everybody had smirked uncomfortably he said, 'I'm a lonely old man but it warms the cockles of my heart to be with people like you.'

Eunice looked euphoric. Frank seemed quite prepared to believe that my father, mother and I lived together happily in that fancy riverside flat. He did not seem to remember that I had been tainted by a deviant school project or even that I had talked about my mother's lodger at the last dinner. If he had taken offence and rushed off to Australia he seemed to be prepared to forgive and forget. We had started afresh. If it weren't for the fact that Eunice and Richard were so smarmy and over the top, their eyebrows constantly dancing up and down like manic puppets, it would have all been quite splendid.

'Louise, this is wonderful,' said Frank, as he finished his last morsel of raspberry tart.

'I didn't make it,' said my mother.

My father waggled his eyebrows at her. 'Louise loves to cook but she's been busy with her charity work.'

'Have I?' asked my mother.

My father smiled a deadly smile. 'You know you have.'

Eunice quickly changed the subject and launched everyone into a discussion on house values in the Chelsea area. My father was happy to go along with that and had a useful twenty minutes talking about his work in buying and selling property. At one point it seemed as if he had almost persuaded Frank to become a partner in one of his enter-

196

prises but Frank halted the conversation when he noticed me on the other side of the table, head down, tucking into second helpings of lemon soufflé and raspberry tart smothered in double cream.

'You're very quiet, Jane. How's the school project?'

'Oh er ...' I said, with a mouth full. 'I'm not doing it. I gave it up.'

'Gave it up?' he seemed astonished. 'Why?'

'I er ... didn't want to ... I had too much other work. Too much homework. Couldn't fit it in.'

Grandma Eunice looked heartily relieved about that, and so did my father.

But my mother looked disturbed. She picked up a fork and began to drum it insistently on the table, very fast, in a little whirring, vibrating kind of way. Everyone looked at her.

My mother's mouth tightened. 'I don't like Jane being made to lie,' she said. 'She's still working on her school project. A young girl should not be made to lie by adults who are only thinking of themselves.'

There was a horrified silence.

'And while we're at it,' she went on, 'I don't live in this flat. I live in a basement in Shepherd's Bush with a paying lodger. I am by profession a washerwoman. I've been divorced and living apart from Richard for over six years. My mother has had five husbands and she's worried about paying her mortgage. That's us in a nutshell.'

The horrified silence grew more horrified.

My other stood up. 'Come on, Jane, we're going home. I'm sorry about this, Frank. You're a lamb led to the slaughter.'

I grabbed a handful of After Eights and some little Swiss wafers from a silver platter on the side table and followed my mother. I was really pleased that she didn't use her killer instinct until after I'd had second helpings of pudding.

*

We caught a bus home. My mother sat staring at her reflection in the window, and her reflection, in its icy pearls and navy-blue velvet, stared back at her in cool approval.

'That was brilliant,' I said. 'That was the killer instinct. That was absolutely brilliant!' I was delighted to have discovered that she could use this killer instinct on someone besides me.

My mother and her reflection continued to stare at each other, while traffic lights flashed on and off and the intersections at the Kings Road and then the Fulham Road came and went behind the transparent face with the pearls.

'Do you think you could use it on Vincent now?' I asked hopefully. 'Could you say, "Get lost, Vincent, you fat freak. And while we're at it, double my wages, no, triple them, you stingy weirdo."?'

My mother finally dismissed her reflection and turned to me. 'Do you think Frank stayed for coffee?'

I tried to imagine the scene in that dining-room after we walked out. What happened to those flabbergasted faces, those dropped jaws? I couldn't. I couldn't see anything. 'I don't know.'

'No, neither do I.'

'But,' I said with a certain amount of alarm. 'People with the killer instinct don't worry about what happens after they leave the room. You shouldn't be asking things like that. You have to tread over your victims' bodies and move on. Do you think Clint Eastwood worries about someone he's shot?'

When we got home we found Freddy flopped on the floor in his bedsocks watching *Newsnight* and eating, in contrast to our sumptuous meal, Welsh rarebit. We told him about my mother's remarkable explosion but he was not convinced that it was a genuine demonstration of the killer instinct.

'All those classes have made you bad-tempered, that's all,'

he said. 'If that guy had punched you on the nose regularly for several weeks it would have had the same effect.'

My mother looked disappointed. 'Are you saying it was just a fit of bad temper?'

I was fascinated to observe how the hot cheese on Freddy's toast bubbled and rippled enticingly with tasty little rivulets dribbling across the plate. 'Could I have a taste, Freddy?' I asked.

'No, you can't,' said my mother. 'You've eaten enough.'

'See, Freddy,' I said despairingly. 'She's bossy with me now. Isn't that the killer instinct?'

'I don't think so. The killer instinct means you become very successful. It doesn't mean you shout at people.'

My mother looked confused. 'Maybe I should phone Arnold and ask him if it is the killer instinct. He would know.'

'Arnold?' I asked. 'When did you start calling him Arnold?'

Freddy shook his head. 'Don't ask him. He'll say it's the killer instinct. Well he would, wouldn't he? That's what he's selling. If it's really the killer instinct you'll start being really successful, and it won't wear off. If it's just a fit of bad temper brought on by stress you'll get over it eventually.'

'You mean,' said my mother, 'that this will go and I'll be the same as I always was?' The idea really depressed her.

'Well how do you feel?' asked Freddy. 'Do you feel like you want to conquer the world?'

My mother looked questioningly at her bony, overworked hands, which were no different from the way they had always looked and offered no clues. 'I don't know. Is conquering the world a worthwhile goal?'

'That's a hard question,' said Freddy, taking another bite of his Welsh rarebit.

'She shouldn't be asking questions like that,' I said.

'People with the killer instinct don't worry about whether it's right to do things. I keep on telling her that.' I picked a crumb of melted cheese off Freddy's plate.

'See that,' said Freddy. 'The kid's a vulture.'

'Does that mean I have the killer instinct?' I asked hopefully.

'No. It means you're a vulture. You wait for other people to do all the work and then you help yourself. Vultures are the scum of the earth.'

'I think you're overreacting. I only took a crumb.'

'Let's talk about me,' said my mother, her face getting really pink as the events of the evening finally began to dawn on her. 'Wasn't I absolutely amazing this evening? Did anyone believe I could do it?'

Freddy picked his plate off the floor and stood up. 'What about your poor mother? You've ruined her life. She wanted to marry that rich old man and now she doesn't have a hope in hell.'

My mother's face dropped. 'Oh dear,' she said.

'Ha,' Freddy said to me. 'Look at that. She hasn't changed.'

And, up to a point, I had to agree with him.

SEX 2000 – CONSUMER REPORT

How ignorant are parents about their children's sexual activity?

'It's another difficult subject,' I moaned to Sophia just before our history teacher, Miss Collins, came into the classroom.

'No it's not. Who have you asked so far?'

'Harriet and Berenice.' They were two almost friendly girls who had not made it into any élite groups but were hoping to make it. They were nervous about being seen talking to me as it could have ruined their chances.

'Harriet and Berenice have absolutely no sexual activity to hide from their parents,' sneered Sophia. 'They can't afford to admit it to you. They're trying to get in with Didi.' Didi was in a gang of out and out slags, who despised inexperienced women.

'So who should I ask?'

'Ask anybody for God's sake. You picked the two most inexperienced girls in the class.'

Sophia went over to a group of girls in the corner of the classroom and said, 'How much do you let your parents know about your sex life?' Then she signalled to me to bring my tape recorder over.

They all talked at once so it was hard to record.

'You never give even the smallest tidbit to a parent. I never tell them anything, and we even argue about that. I hate my parents.' It was very fashionable then to hate your parents.

'I never discuss anything with my parents.'

'Parents are paranoid enough already. You don't tell them anything.'

'My parents have got a pretty good idea about it. They did the same thing, but they just did it later than us.'

'My parents know what goes on. They just think I don't have anything to do with it because I'm sensible.'

'If you want to get off with your boyfriend you go round to a friend's house.'

'Don't leave a condom in a friend's bed. It's really tacky.'

'Brenda did that to me.'

'Where were your parents?'

'Gone to see *Hamlet*.'

'You can't tell a parent anything. If one parent finds out, then the word gets round. Parents are always trying to get clues from each other.'

'If they find out anything I get grounded. Telling parents is a one-way ticket to jail as far as I'm concerned.'

'Watch out. Jane's recording.'

'Jane! You absolute cow! Don't tell Mrs Cassels.'

I discussed it with Sophia later.

'I would hate it if some girl came round with her boyfriend and did it in my bed, or on my side of the bed, I only have half a bed. But I'd hate it if they did it near my Teddy Bears and my cat and my little blanket.'

Sophia had another of her rare sympathetic moments. 'The solution to that problem is to put your Teddy Bears etcetera in the other room so they won't be shocked.'

'Yes I suppose so. But finding a wet soggy condom, full of yuk . . . oh yuk!'

Sophia, amusing herself I'm sure, continued to be sympathetic. 'You'd have to carry out an exorcism and remove all the hot breathy sex from your sweet little room.'

'How would I do that?'

Sophia thought about it. 'You could wave all your Winnie the Pooh books round the room and chant, 'Away with wicked desire. Pooh reigns.' And then hurl the condom out into the street and hope it won't hit a passing old lady.'

Conclusion: Young people must be extremely secretive about sex. (1) With their friends they have to pretend to be experienced when they're not, and (2) with their parents they have to pretend to be inexperienced when they're not. Parents have very set ideas, learned in the sixties, about when and if their children should start on sex, alcohol and drugs. It is important to keep these parents happy and let them stick to their imaginary schedule.

CHAPTER

23

It was one of those bright cold days that England is so good at. The sky was a smart, new blue, tautly stretched out over Shepherd's Bush and well lit by a hidden but obviously friendly sun. My mother and I paid no heed to the stained pavements blotted with residues of last night's drunken indiscretions, and set out at a good clip to Vincent's Coachworks, as we were late.

When we arrived the workmen in the alley were all gathered at the back of the site so we did not have to put up with their catcalls, which made a nice change. But further up the alley was Vincent, scowling rudely at us as he checked a smashed window on a customer's Audi. 'You're late, Louise. You'll get the old heave-ho my girl if you don't get out of bed earlier in the morning.'

My mother looked at Vincent and I watched her carefully to see if her face had a killer look, but it didn't. It had more of a pleasant, Mona Lisa type expression. She looked at him for a second and then went into the office, just as a customer was leaving.

Dolores, in a leopard-print shirt, was behind the counter exuding fifteen different fragrances. 'Oh, Louise. You're late! There's already a couple of service washes to do. You'd better get in there. And Vincent wants the floor mopped. It

203

didn't get done last night. Hup hup hup!'

She was waving the form that the departing customer had filled out, waving it in the direction of the filing cabinet, in a haphazard, spoiled for choice manner. Her hand eventually settled like an alighting butterfly on the H section.

'What was the customer's name?' asked my mother.

'Shipley.'

'Then why are you putting it there?' asked my mother.

Dolores looked up sharply. 'Because I am. What's it to you?'

'The customer was called Shipley. Put it under S.'

'He had a Honda,' replied Dolores, looking very testy indeed.

To avoid further argument my mother went over, took the form out of Dolores' hand, and filed it under S.

'Who do you think you are?' asked Dolores, thoroughly peeved. She took the form out of the S file and put it under H. 'Stupid cow.'

'Dolores,' said my mother very sharply. 'Putting it under H is like putting it in a black hole. The customer's name is Shipley, it goes under S and nothing else. You're not consistent. Sometimes you put a Honda Civic under C or a Honda Accord under A. You don't know how to file things. You're useless. In fact you're worse than useless. You make me a lot of hard work.'

She took the form out of the H file and put it back under S.

'Well pardon me for living,' said Dolores. She was just about to flare up. I'd seen her do it with Vincent. She could be a very nasty piece of work once she got going.

My mother put her bag on the counter and took her coat off decisively, like someone preparing for a punch up. 'I think I'll stay here today, Dolores. I can't go on letting you ruin my filing system. It takes me all week to put it right.'

Dolores went on being about to flare up. The surprise element, the fact that she never in a million years would have expected so much as a peep out of my mother, was delaying her explosion. Her bottom lip shaped itself into the beginning of various vowel sounds but none came out.

My mother, however, went on. 'You've had your fun in the office, Dolores. But now it's over. Go and do the service washes. It'll be a useful experience for you if you want to know about Vincent's business. You can think about whether we're charging enough. Off you go.'

Dolores' bottom lip finally curled into a smile. 'You're joking aren't you? You're kidding. Vincent put you up to it.' She turned to me. 'Did Vincent put your mum up to this?'

I shook my head. 'No.'

Dolores looked deflated. 'Hah,' she said, letting her last bit of air out.

My mother moved behind the counter and began shoving Dolores' knick-knacks towards the wall. Dolores watched her in dumb fascination. My mother looked up. 'Don't just stand there, Dolores. The service washes are building up. You know what a tough day Saturday is.'

At that moment Vincent walked in, slapping his hand threateningly with a big spanner. 'Hey droopy drawers,' he said to my mother. 'One more late arrival like that and you're out of here.'

'Vincent,' said Dolores. 'This stupid cow's told me to go and do the service washes. She won't let me stay in the office.'

'She what?' Vincent stopped slapping. He looked at my mother standing possessively behind the counter, he looked at me trying to be as invisible as possible, and he looked at Dolores who was beginning to look almost tearful. 'She what?'

My mother spoke up. 'I've told her to go and work in the

205

launderette. I don't want her in here mucking up my filing system.'

'You don't want her in here mucking up your filing system?' Vincent repeated, a little vein on his forehead begin to bulge.

'You got it in one,' said my mother. That was one of Dr Jefferies' expressions.

For reasons that I will explain later, some of the things Vincent said subsequently have been expurgated by someone using killer instinct intimidation in the editing of this book. You will have to imagine what he said. It won't take much imagination because Vincent didn't use any. He didn't actually say you dumb little squirt. I put it there to fill in the blanks.

'What's gone wrong with you, you dumb little squirt? Do you think you can walk in here and tell Dolores what to do? Get out of here and go to the launderette, you dumb little squirt.' He banged his big spanner down on the counter and everyone jumped and so did all the knick-knacks.

My mother did not move. She still had that little Mona Lisa smile twitching at the corner of her lips. 'No. You hired me to look after the office. And that's what I'm going to do. I can't do two jobs. And anyway I'm over qualified to be a washerwoman.'

Vincent leaned over the counter and tried to grab my mother. 'Get the hell out of here. Go on get.' (He didn't say hell.)

My mother dodged backwards. 'No. I'm staying here.'

'I said get in that launderette or I'll take you there myself.'

'No you won't. Because if you do I'll sue you for assault.'

'OK, you're fired.'

'No I'm not.'

'I said you're fired.'

'You can't fire me.'

'Why not?'

'Because I'll tell them you're patching up totalled cars you've dragged off scrap heaps, and I'll tell them that you're advertising them in magazines and conning the public.'

'You wouldn't do that.'

'I will if you give me the sack.'

'That's blackmail.'

'Call it what you like. And while you're about it, I want to be paid twice as much. And if you argue about it I'll sue you for back pay. You've been cheating me out of a decent wage for years.'

'You dumb little squirt,' said Vincent, or words to that effect.

At that moment two customers came in, a man and his wife in matching beige corduroy car coats. As they walked up to the counter there was a deadly silence. The customers' footsteps on the hard stone floor made helpless, hollow sounds which reverberated against the brick walls. Vincent, Dolores, my mother and I all watched the unsuspecting two with an intensity that began to make them very uncomfortable.

The man looked at his wife and she looked back. 'Er . . . is this . . . er . . . the office?' inquired the man.

'Yes it is,' said my mother. And she turned to Vincent and Dolores. 'I suggest you two get back to work.'

Dolores sidled over to Vincent, placed one exquisitely fingernailed hand on his fat belly, and whispered, 'She's gone off her rocker.'

'No I haven't,' said my mother. Then she turned to the customers. 'What can I do for you?'

Vincent and Dolores left the battlefield and could be seen huddled together on the other side of the alley next to a pile of crankcases and bumpers. When they came out of the huddle they went off in different directions, Dolores, in her fancy leopard-print, to blood and sweat in the launderette and Vincent, bursting out of his denim overalls, to his wizard's workshop where cars were conjured up from tangled heaps. They avoided my mother for the rest of the day and, if any communications were needed, I was sent as a messenger. I ran from the workshop to the office and back, and from the launderette to the office and back, on an almost constant loop. It was far more exercise than I wanted or expected.

At lunch time my mother closed the office for forty-five minutes and took me out for a sandwich. This was an unheard of treat. My mother usually grabbed her lunch in mouthfuls while she continued to work.

Unfortunately the workmen at the end of the alley were also preparing to have their lunch and were all gathering into an idle, lumpen group at the corner of the site. When my mother and I walked past they all called out and whistled. Owing to the restrictions placed on me I am unable to reproduce exactly what they said. But it was mostly about going to the back of the building site and taking our clothes off.

The one they called John, the rudest of them all, stepped out in his big boots and cement-covered jeans, and wouldn't let us past.

'Get out of the way,' my mother said.

'Oh I can't do that darling,' said John. 'You've got to help me out first.'

'I said get out of the way.'

'Make me.'

My mother considered it.

'No,' I said in a panic. 'Don't.' I knew her martial arts were not nearly good enough yet. So did she.

208

'Well let me see,' said my mother. 'You'll have to help me. Put your foot there.'

Grinning wildly, John put his foot right next to my mother's. All the other workmen jeered and catcalled.

'Now put your shoulder there.'

John bent down, with a lascivious shimmy and put his shoulder at an angle to my mother.

'OK. Give me your hand,' she ordered.

There were hysterically cheerful whistles from all the workmen as John thrust his big, dirty hand towards my mother.

'Now John, lunge forward when I say so. Lunge very hard because I have to use my opponent's force to my own advantage.'

My mother, muttering her teacher's instructions to herself, grasped John's wrist very firmly, and leaned into position as she had been taught.

'Lunge!'

'Go on, John,' yelled his fellow workers. 'Give her a lunge!'

John, still grinning, waved to the crowd and then obediently lunged. For a second my mother staggered under the impact of his huge body, then with an almighty flick she harnessed his force and threw him over her shoulder, sending his feet in a wide arc over his head. John's feet flew through the air in a bizarre somersault and he landed with a thud behind her on his back.

The whistling and the jeering stopped. John lay silent and winded on the hard concrete, staring up in bewilderment like an overturned turtle.

There was a silence. It seemed as if my mother was leaving a trail of silences in her wake. She stared down at the workman's unmoving, prostrate body, and gave it a small kick.

'Get up. Wakey wakey.'

The she turned and lead me down the alley to a sandwich bar round the corner where we celebrated. It was a truly momentous occasion because we had never been in a local sandwich bar before. This particular one had torn plastic table tops and chipped chairs, but we were enchanted.

'Ham and cheese, Jane?' said my mother, smiling as I'd never seen her smile before.

'Yes, please, and salami if they've got it.'

'One ham and cheese, with salami if you've got it, and one tuna,' ordered my mother rhapsodically. Turning to me she said, 'It was cheating to ask him to lunge. But I couldn't have done it without him doing a really good lunge, and he did a terrific one. And let's face it. The killer instinct is about cheating when you can.'

'If it is only a fit of bad temper,' I mused, 'you should probably make a list of important things to do before it wears off.'

My mother's smile drooped a little. 'Do you think I'm like Cinderella with the glass slipper? It all goes at midnight?'

'I hope not.'

She looked around the crowded sandwich bar. 'Well I'm going to enjoy it while I can. Isn't this the most amazing place? Now we're finding out how the other half lives. People take lunch breaks every day. See. Look at their faces. They don't think it's special. I feel sorry for them really. They're not enjoying it nearly as much as I am.'

After our sandwich we went for a little walk, another unheard of activity. We went through the market and enjoyed the sunshine, the brightly coloured fabrics on the stalls and the throngs of Saturday people. It was a day of great events. Never to be forgotten. Historic. What a day.

*

Freddy, of course, was still sceptical. When we came home he was ironing his shirt, in preparation for an evening's work as a photographer at a twenty-first birthday party.

'There's no way of knowing why you're behaving like this,' he said, curving his iron carefully around the shirt collar. 'It could be a total mental breakdown, the loss of all your reasoning faculties. You could be bonkers. Or it could be a mental blip. By Monday you could be the same as you always were. There's absolutely no way of knowing now.'

'You're so depressing, Freddy,' moaned my mother.

'No. I'm the voice of caution. We've been over this before. Don't get your heart set on being a killer for the rest of your life.' Freddy held up his shirt and examined it for wrinkles. The party was going to be at the Carleton Towers, not a place for wrinkles.

'I'm seeing Arnold tonight. He'll know if it's going to last.'

'Arnold?' I said suspiciously. 'Why do you keep on calling him Arnold?'

'Why not?' said my mother in a self-conscious voice.

'Oh my God!' said Freddy.

'What?' asked my mother.

'Oh my God!'

'What?'

'He's been screwing you. He's had his way . . . That's not a good idea, Louise.'

My mother, head bowed, was examining her hands with an intensity that denoted only one thing.

'I said that's not a good idea,' repeated Freddy.

She was offended. Her head came up just enough for her to look Freddy in the eye. 'What's so terrible?'

'What's so terrible? He should know better, that's what.

211

You're a patient. He's a psychologist. You're weak. And he's taken advantage. What a creep.'

'Hmpff,' she said.

I was outraged. 'How could you? How could you with Dr Jefferies?'

'He's not a monster.' My mother looked like a hurt child.

'That's not the point, Louise,' said Freddy, putting on his shirt. 'In a patient–client relationship it's not ethical. Patients, especially a patient like you, are incredibly vulnerable.'

'How do you know I didn't throw myself at him?'

'Even if you did it wouldn't make any difference. When you're a doctor you don't do it with a patient. There are limits and that's one of them. He knows it. I've got to go. Now tell this guy to let you down lightly. I don't want any broken hearts around here. My life is tough enough as it is. I don't want another mess to clear up. Do you hear me? Stop it. And take up knitting.'

Freddy grabbed a jacket and his camera equipment and flew out of the door leaving me staring accusingly at my mother.

'How could you? With Dr Jefferies of all people?'

My mother hung her head. 'I'm sorry, Jane. But he's ... well we've been practically living together for months. I've had all those classes ...'

'That's no excuse.'

'I'm sorry.'

'It's ruined my day.'

'I'm sorry.'

'It's no good saying sorry. It shouldn't have happened. Not with Dr Jefferies.'

My mother was chewing her lip. 'Would you like me to make you some cocoa?'

'No.'

It was becoming very clear to me that people said one thing about sex and did another. Dr Jefferies had given me all that guff about how we'd be better off without sex and how it was just mythology. And how everyone made too much fuss about it. And here he was seducing my mother in an extremely unethical way.

And she, who'd always said she couldn't even remember sex, was acting as though she certainly did remember and had chosen it for its positive benefits. She was even finding it difficult to be ashamed of herself. I could tell a performance from the real thing.

And Freddy was perhaps the greatest mystery of all. He'd said sex was life and happiness and pleasure and that he wasn't a great one for holding back the tide. He'd been so gung ho and now here he was being really shocked that my mother had actually gone out and done it. It just didn't make any sense.

How was I expected to come up with any clear conclusions for my consumer survey if everyone was so changeable? It was a mess.

My mother was shifting from one foot to another. 'Oh. Well I better be going then. Will you be all right on your own?'

'No. I'll be haunted by terrible thoughts.'

'Then do you want to come with me? You can sit with Mrs Moon and discuss her visits to the whelk stall.'

'No. I'm too shocked. I can't believe it after what Dr Jefferies said about sex. He said there wasn't even such a thing as a sexual instinct. He said he could teach people to overcome sex. He's a phoney.'

My mother slunk away, her glorious day ending under a black cloud and her killer instinct trailing in tatters behind her.

*

SEX 2000 – CONSUMER REPORT

Why do people say one thing about sex and do another?

On Sunday, a rainy, miserable day, I set out to confront Dr Jefferies. I took the last remaining umbrella from our flat, a tatty thing with bent spokes and spaces where there should have been umbrella. It caught the wind and turned inside out with an infuriating frequency, which made me scream at it. Life was getting me down. I couldn't rely on anything, not even an umbrella.

Dr Jefferies, in a grey shirt and grey pullover, muted tones, seemed prepped for my visit.

'You've come to complain,' he said as he opened the front door. And as I looked around for the familiar stout figure he added, 'I've managed to get rid of Mrs Moon. Only temporarily, but it gives us a little privacy.'

Surely Mrs Moon, arch sleuth, would have picked up any hints of sexual misbehaviour. 'Doesn't she know about you and my mother?' I asked accusingly.

Dr Jefferies tried a casual smile but it didn't work. Instead he bared his teeth. 'Amazing as it may seem, no she doesn't. Your mother and I've avoided any swinging from the chandeliers.'

I winced, finding that remark extremely painful. I was, and still am, at the age when the idea of one's parent doing anything other than being a parent was simply not nice.

I followed Dr Jefferies across the hall into the kitchen. 'We have the kitchen to ourselves now that nosey old bat's cleared off,' he said. 'Would you like a cup of tea?'

'No I don't drink tea.' I wasn't going to encourage him by drinking any of his tea. He was a sinner.

'Orange juice, coke, apple juice?'

With considerable self-control I managed a sullen, 'No

thank you'. The nerve of the man, expecting me to drink his tainted liquids.

'Well you won't mind if I heat up some coffee. I'm a coffee addict.'

He would be an addict wouldn't he. 'No,' I said. 'Go ahead.'

I waited with a pinched, disapproving face as he heated up his addictive brew.

'I expect you hope it chokes me,' he said as he poured it into a cup.

He took the words right out of my mouth. 'No,' I said.

We sat down at the kitchen table. 'OK. Lay it on me. What have I done wrong?'

What had he done wrong? How could he ask that? What about ethics? What about everything he'd said to me? I hardly knew where to begin.

'You told me that sex was something we learned, sort of like the killer instinct,' I said, my voice trembling with all my pent-up outrage. 'You said it was mythology. You acted as though you were above it. But you're not.'

'Well,' he said, looking philosophical, 'I guess one of the first things you learn about sex is that it's undeniably a social act. No man is an island.'

I stared at him fiercely. If he thought he could get out of it by speechifying then he had another think coming.

But he certainly tried. He ran his fingers through his untidy, tufty hair, took a good swig of coffee and launched forth. 'Yes. Every act of sex, however secretive, is somehow written in the sky for us all to see. I should have remembered that.'

'I don't think you should have done that to my mother.'

He had the decency to look hurt and paused to remove his rimless glasses and polished them with a piece of shirt dug out from his belt. 'I didn't *do* it to her. She's not

215

helpless. She can make her own decisions.'

'Well even if she can, why did you do it?'

He looked reflectively at his knees. 'There are various kinds of sexual activity, and this particular one sprang out of extremely stressful circumstances.'

'Yes. But you said sex could be conquered. Why didn't you conquer it?'

'Usually I do. But your mother is a very unusual woman. And I guess I just wasn't prepared for that. And ... and ... there are times when you begin to notice qualities in someone. You begin to admire the human spirit. You develop an affection for it. And you want to get close to that person.'

'It doesn't have to be sex though does it? There's all sorts of ways of getting close to someone besides sex if what you say is true.'

'Shall I be honest?'

'Yes.'

'Your mother was beginning to get independent. And I wanted to, like, to lasso her. And I ... poor mortal that I am ... couldn't think of any other way to pin her down ... as it were.'

'Does that mean you like her?'

'Oh yes. I like her.'

'Oh.' I thought about that, then I said. 'If you really liked her you wouldn't have done that to her.'

'Well I've done it now. I can't take it back. And the most important thing about sex is not to let it dominate your life. And one of the ways it does that is by making you feel guilty.'

'But you should feel guilty. She's a patient and you're a doctor. Freddy says that's terrible.'

Dr Jefferies stood up, walked around the kitchen table in a chastened pilgrimage and then sat down again. He breathed a deep sigh. 'Freddy's got a big mouth. I've heard a lot about Freddy from your mother.'

'Well what are you going to do about it?'

'Do about it? Nothing. And you know what? I'm going to go on being friendly with your mother.'

'*Being friendly*?' I said with alarm.

'What's wrong with that? She's not a patient anyway. If she's anything she's a student. A mature student. And I like her and she likes me.'

'No she doesn't, she said she wanted to kill you.'

'Has she said that this week?'

'Not this week.'

'There you go.'

I sat there with my lower lip thrust forth, feeling thoroughly let down by all humanity.

'Life's tough.' Dr Jefferies took off his glasses again and polished them with another piece of his shirt. They were getting a more than thorough cleaning. 'We all grow up being told sex is irresistible and then we're told to resist it.'

'You didn't did you?' I said spitefully.

Dr Jefferies' eyes, without glasses, looked like soft molluscs that had lost their shell. 'You know,' he said as he put his glasses on again, 'you're very protective of your mother, but you don't have to be any more. She's changed.'

'I thought she'd changed. But when she told me about what you'd done to her, then I thought no, she's just giving in to some pushy person the way she always has.'

Dr Arnold Jefferies stood up again or rather he rose up like some giant sea creature emerging out of the waves. He was asserting his authority over a mere whiffet of a person such as myself. 'I think we've chewed this over as much as we'll ever do. You'd better go home. I have a lot to do.'

I got up and walked slowly out of the kitchen and down the hall to the front door. I felt a small sense of relief. At least I had annoyed him, I had inflicted a degree of punishment.

He opened the door with far more enthusiasm to let me out than he had to let me in. In fact he swept it open. Whoosh. I half expected him to kick my backside and send me rolling into the street.

'I'll say one last thing,' he said in a killer instinct, believe-this-or-die voice. 'The sexual act, in and of itself, doesn't begin to, it doesn't even touch on the depth and breadth and the whole universe of interchange that goes on between a man and a woman. What goes on, nobody really knows, it's an everlasting secret.'

'OK,' I said and ran down the steps, along the street and away.

I left him there waiting for something. What was it? Applause? Well he was not going to get it from me. He may have bamboozled my mother but he would not bamboozle me.

It seemed to me that he was making one last attempt to appear less guilty and I certainly was not going to let him off the hook.

Conclusion: People say one thing about sex and do another because they forget what they said about it. This is because sexual activity destroys those brain cells used in memory retention.

CHAPTER
24

Word got out about my mother having learned the killer instinct. It got out because Dr Jefferies put it about. There were a lot of pictures in the newspapers of Dr Jefferies standing with his arm around my mother smiling triumphantly, while she also smiled out triumphantly from underneath his arm. He was much taller than her.

A couple of photographers even went to Vincent's Coachworks and Launderette and took photos of my mother with Vincent and somehow Dolores squeezed herself into one of the photographs. She had rushed hotfoot from her hairdresser's salon in Ealing, where she was supposed to be working every weekday. Vincent and Dolores were both quoted as saying how pleased they were now my mother had the killer instinct, how they had really wanted her to have it for years, and felt so sorry the way she suffered being a complete worm most of her life.

Freddy kept on waiting for the killer instinct to disappear. He would try being really bossy to see if my mother would sink back into being her old loser self. But she insisted that she did not have to use the killer instinct if someone was only *pretending* to be bossy. So if Freddy shouted at her, 'Woman, bring me some clean socks,' she would go and get them because she said he didn't really mean it. Freddy said that was a very fine philosophical point. He and I would argue about it for hours. The topic of the debate: When is the killer instinct not the killer instinct?

Grandma Eunice had sent my mother to Coventry and was not phoning, which, as Freddy frequently said, was a blessed relief. However once my mother's photograph appeared in the *Daily Express*, Grandma Eunice claimed all the credit for my mother's dramatic change.

She was on the phone immediately. 'I've been trying to get you to change for years. I'm thrilled that you finally listened to what I've been saying for so long. It's so hard to see a child suffer the way you have, Louise. What a wonderful transformation.'

And when my father saw an article about killer instinct practices in the business world in the *Financial Times* with a smiling photograph of my mother alongside it, he phoned up immediately and asked if my mother would come to a political dinner with him. 'It's black tie. You'll need a long dress. I like sequins if you can get some.'

My mother declined the invitation, giving the same reasons she had before. She had done a lot of work with Dr Jefferies on the broken record technique, where she learned to say the same thing to someone every time they made the same suggestions. People who don't have the killer instinct, for some reason, think they have to think up a new excuse every time.

And even Frank, the elusive millionaire, the big fish who'd swum away down the stream, phoned. 'My dear, I saw your photo in the paper. I realise now what you were doing at that dinner party. Wonderful shock tactics. I'm impressed. We didn't have that kind of training available in my day. Perhaps I could take you to lunch at the Savoy and you could tell me how you did it. Bring your mother if you like.'

'What about me?' I asked. 'Didn't he invite me? Doesn't he know I'm very fond of eating?'

'No,' said my mother. 'He didn't invite you.'

Just like that. Before she would have worried about my feeling hurt, panic would come into her eyes at the mere idea that I might feel deprived, but now it was just, 'No he didn't invite you.' I had come to rely on my mother caring enormously about my every whim. She had never been able to do anything about my whims but she had cared about them. Now she could do something about them but she had put them on the back burner. Freddy said it was very good for my character but of course, Freddy would say that. Frankly, a little indulgence, a few dispensations for someone like myself, who'd had so much to cope with for so long, would not have gone amiss.

There was a party atmosphere around my mother, an aura of success, but I felt I was not part of it. She had the killer instinct and it meant I had to spend more time in the kitchen instead of lounging about. It meant I had to go to the shops far more often whereas before I could have always said, 'You go.' It meant I had to watch less television and eat fewer biscuits and more salads, even watercress. It meant pulling my weight, something I had always avoided with great skill and many tricks honed over the years. I was certainly pleased that my mother was not a total crumb any more, but it was clear to me that I had not thought the whole thing through. I should have realised what I was letting myself in for when I sent my mother to acquire this hitherto exotic, unknown instinct.

I wanted to learn the killer instinct too but Freddy said I didn't need it. He said I would whine my way to the top of any organisation. He said my whining was a really nasty weapon, it would break down barriers merely because people would be dying for me to shut up.

My mother achieved a high degree of fame when she went on breakfast television with Dr Jefferies. She looked extremely smart in an ensemble she had chosen herself in Beauchamp Place and which was paid for by her new boyfriend, the highly immoral Dr Jefferies.

The interviewer was subjected to all kinds of killer instinct tactics by Dr Jefferies, so that within two minutes he, the interviewer that is, was waving a copy of *The Killer Instinct and You* at the camera and exhorting all viewers to buy it.

All was going very well until Dr Jefferies said that the killer instinct, although not an instinct, was the most important factor in anyone's life.

'No it's not,' said my mother.

'Yes it is,' said Dr Jefferies.

'No it's not,' said my mother. 'It's worthless if you don't have some good ideas behind it. In fact it's more than worthless, it's a very dangerous thing to teach to someone who's going to use it badly.'

Dr Jefferies gave my mother a shifty look and then he tried one of his unsuccessful smiles. 'What did I tell you?' he said to the interviewer. 'I've taught her too well. She's using it on me.'

My mother did not crack a smile. 'It's not a laughing matter,' she said. 'It's really sad that anyone should have to learn something with no social value like a killer instinct. We should have advanced beyond it by now. What about kindness?'

Dr Jefferies' eyebrows quivered. 'Kindness? What kindness? The world is a cesspool.'

'The killer instinct is no goal for a thinking person. There are too many people who have it already. It's a problem, not a solution.'

At that moment Dr Jefferies took my mother's hand which was out of view of the camera and squeezed it very hard. In retaliation she kicked his ankle. His wince of pain was extremely visible and looked like an inexplicable, surreal act to anyone watching the programme.

After the show they had a gigantic row which was witnessed by everyone in the television studio. My mother and Dr Jefferies shouted abuse at each other as they walked out of the studio and went to the car park, where my mother refused to get into his car. She went out on to the street where she was kerb-crawled by a screaming Dr Jefferies until she hailed a taxi and jumped in. She lost him in heavy traffic.

'It was cathartic,' my mother said afterwards. 'I've been wanting to tell him what to do with his killer instinct for a long time. A man of his abilities should not be wasting his time on a third-rate thing like that.'

Freddy said that when total losers like my mother learned the killer instinct they used it to force everyone into becoming losers like themselves. 'She's going to force everyone into being kind and thoughtful. They'll all be saying, "After you", "No, after you". Getting through a door will be a nightmare.'

'Freddy,' said my mother, 'you put too much of your energy into perverse arguments.'

After the media had lost interest in the bust-up in the television studio and the phone stopped ringing we had relative peace in our flat. My mother was no longer in communication with Dr Jefferies, and was not attending her Back up and Top up killer instinct classes.

Out of boredom she attended a few political get togethers with my father and began to talk about 'how to capture the public's imagination' and 'future goals for Britain'. She began reading political journals and to theorise about practicality versus ethics in government.

Freddy and I were obliged to read political journals and study the heavy newspapers in order to make sure we understood what she was talking about.

As usual with my mother's extra-curricular activities it meant that the eating of food became a factor of extremely low importance and the meals she threw on the table continued to be really awful.

SEX 2000 – CONSUMER REPORT

Is sex just too much?

Sophia informed me, 'In order for a woman to feel pleasure during sex she has to imagine herself being raped by a gang of men.'

'Yuk!' I said.

'Jane, that's life,' Sophia said sternly. 'Get with the programme.'

'Who said you had to imagine that?'

'It's general knowledge.'

'I'm not going to think that. I refuse.'

'Then you won't have any pleasure. The first time you do it with a boy, he's enough because you're just worried about getting it over and done with. And the second time he's enough, I suppose, but after that you get bored and you have to imagine another boy. Then you have to imagine more and more until eventually you have a whole army of men.'

'A whole army!' I was horrified. 'I absolutely refuse to imagine that.'

'Tut, tut. What about sexual satisfaction, Jane?'

'I don't want it. I refuse to imagine a whole army of men. Doing it is bad enough.'

'You'll be frustrated.'

'So what? I'm not going to think all that junk. I'd much rather be frustrated.'

'OK. Whatever you say.'

'If you have to imagine an army of men leaping about doing disgusting things then personally I'm joining another human race. I'd rather be happy than satisfied.'

'OK. Keep your hair on, Jane.'

'If an army of men tried to get into my imagination and wanted to rape me I'd imagine a machine gun and I'd shoot them all before they got their trousers down. And then they'd never dare to get in my imagination again.'

'OK, OK. Calm down. I'll tell you another Winnie the Pooh story. Do you remember when Pooh was taking a jar of honey to Eeyore? What was it for?'

'It was for Eeyore's birthday.'

'And what did Pooh say to himself when he stopped on the way?'

'Now then Pooh, time for a little something.'

'And then he sat down and dipped his paw in and he ate some honey didn't he?'

'Yes.'

'And then what happened?'

'He finished off the whole jar and there was none left for Eeyore's birthday.'

'Right. Now do you feel a little better?'

'A bit.'

Conclusion: Sex can require enormous efforts of imagination which can be beyond the capacities of some people.

CHAPTER

25

Grandma Eunice's marriage to Frank Sherman came just in the nick of time as she had defaulted on the last four monthly mortgage payments and the building society was getting very stroppy.

How did she pull it off after so many setbacks? Everyone had a different explanation. Freddy said it was utterly without an explanation because it was not humanly possible for any man in his right mind to want to marry Grandma Eunice. My father said it was a brilliant act of seduction by someone totally lacking in seductive powers, a miraculous example of the thinnest of human resources being stretched to their utmost. And Aunt Joanna said Frank must have been far more lonely than any of us realised.

My mother told me that there was nothing miraculous about it because Eunice had used a killer instinct technique to get Frank to propose to her. She got it out of Chapter 4 of *The Killer Instinct and You*, a book she had been studying avidly ever since my mother's photo started appearing in the papers. During their lunch at the Savoy Grill, Grandma Eunice kept on saying that destiny was slipping through Frank's fingers and what a tragedy that would be for everyone concerned.

'A basic sales technique,' my mother called it, 'blatant but effective. You'd be amazed how terrified people get over the idea of a missed opportunity.'

That was not an explanation as far as I was concerned. I thought my mother showed a naïve trust in all the killer instinct principles. There was no reason on God's earth why a rich, handsome man like Frank would sacrifice himself to Grandma Eunice. Personally I put it down to something more sinister like witchcraft. Somewhere eye of toad and a bat's wing or two had entered into the equation.

The wedding cost Frank a pretty penny. At the reception, which was held at the gloating bride's house, there were curried chicken balls, smoked salmon and shrimp vol au vents as well as caviare and oysters. There was a really good chocolate almond torte served with either double cream or Häagen-Dazs ice-cream, as well as three different kinds of cheesecake, a charlotte russe and a lemon mousse with a caramel sauce. I can vouch that they were all excellent.

Grandma Eunice wore a cream lace dress which made her look like a bathroom window, according to Freddy. Frank Sherman beamed happily over the entire proceedings and showed no awareness of the fact that he'd got an extremely bad deal.

The event was made uncomfortable for me by the sudden and unexpected appearance of Garvie, who waited mournfully across the street on his bicycle, and it was made uncomfortable for my mother by Dr Jefferies who parked his car near Garvie's bicycle. The two of them did their sad, neglected dogs left outside a supermarket act, and tried to make us feel sorry for them.

'What are we going to do?' I asked my mother.

'Leave them there, of course,' she said in that heartless way of hers.

'But it's cold,' I said.

'Tough,' said my mother.

I could not be distracted from my main goal of the afternoon which was collecting together a doggie bag of things I planned to eat later. Due to its size it was more of a doggie suitcase but I had to work fast, especially with the chocolate torte, as everybody was having second helpings, and there was a distinct danger there would be none left for me to take away.

Frank made a speech saying how happy he was to have such a beautiful new bride, and he said it without choking. Grandma Eunice grinned and grinned and several of Frank's relatives mosied about suspiciously asking why they had married in such a hurry. 'I don't think she's pregnant,' I told one of them.

My father made a speech, although he had no right to whatsoever, but he wanted to get up and spout. It was the champagne talking.

'Let's drink to the happy couple,' he said, twitching his shiny pink nose. 'Let me not to the marriage of true minds admit impediment,' and he beamed at everyone in a meaningful way. 'They're an example to us all of the triumph of patience over adversity. Eunice knew that if she waited long enough she'd win. We didn't think she had a hope in hell but she hung in there. Here's to an amazingly resourceful woman.'

All the wedding guests raised their glasses to an amazingly resourceful woman, all that is apart from Frank's suspicious relatives. They began to whisper things about prenuptial agreements. But as Eunice so sensibly pointed out, 'It's too late for that now.'

To prevent my father making any more speeches, my mother stood up. 'I have an announcement to make,' she said. 'I've been asked to stand as a prospective parliamentary candidate at the next election.'

Everyone cheered. My father looked a little crestfallen and

obviously wished he had never invited my mother along to any of his functions.

As if on cue, Dr Arnold Jefferies strolled in through the front door and stood alongside my mother accepting the cheers with her, even bowing a little. 'Thank you, thank you,' he said. 'Louise will make a perfect candidate. She has what it takes. You see before you, ladies and gentlemen, the next prime minister!' And he grabbed her hand and held it aloft like a prizefighter's and everyone cheered and cheered. There were a few seconds when it looked as though my mother was about to punch Dr Jefferies on the nose but she decided against it. And you could say that was a moment of reconciliation, and the official moment when Dr Jefferies took over from my father in my mother's life.

I felt rather sorry for Garvie hanging around outside missing all the festivities, so I invited him in for some lemon mousse and ice-cream which he wolfed down in no seconds flat. Then he worked his way slowly through everything on the buffet table. I knew he did it because he had nothing to say but I was used to that by now.

An experienced woman understands those sort of things.

My mother did not lose her killer instinct. As proof of this you only have to read this book. When I first wrote it there were bucket loads of swear words in all reported speech and she went through my manuscript and scratched them all out. She took no heed of the fact that, in the closing years of this century, school girls are using more swear words than most people realise and most adults swear a lot too.

She said that a book is an example and I said it was holding a mirror up to nature with all its faults. She said that a book is a microcosm locked in time and stays there, watched and read and becomes magnified. Therefore swear words should be used more sparingly than they are in life and this would act as an encouragement to people to stop using them and think up more inventive insults and exclamations of surprise.

As she was the one with the killer instinct, I had to give in.

SEX 2000 – CONSUMER REPORT

The final conclusion.

Although it was the last day of term and a lot of people were planning to bunk off they all decided to stay and hear my Sex 2000 final report. This was proof that sex really gets attention. No wonder people use it when they can't think up a good idea.

The day before, Sophia had presented her Travel 2000 report and everyone had practically fallen asleep, including Sophia. Her research was atrociously thin; she had been saying all term that she would use personal experience as the basis of her research. But how much can you glean from a daily bus ride?

I think Mrs Cassels had deliberately put my report on the last afternoon of the last day, relying on the supposition that a good portion of the class would have scattered to the winds by then. But she had not taken into account the drawing power of sex. I had a full house.

I read out my interviews and conclusions, abbreviated for presentation. There were a few snickers, especially during the section about deceiving parents, but everyone went very quiet and stared at their desk when I read the interview about the blow job. Mrs Cassels went rather tense too.

For my conclusion I said, 'I would not recommend sex as a useful consumer item as it is not user friendly. The consumer cannot be guaranteed satisfaction or lasting performance. Even consumers who insist that they are fully satisfied with this product do not actually seem to be all that satisfied. It seems to live largely in the imagination of the consumer and requires a great deal of constant topping up by an assortment of putrid or preposterous thoughts. It cannot be advertised correctly in a sales catalogue as people are very dishonest when they describe it. In the olden days most people were dishonest in pretending that they had nothing to do with sex. Now they pretend that it is the best and most wonderful thing in the entire world and that to go on about sex all the time is really noble and good. I think that in the next century our generation should revolutionise the marketing of this product, if they can figure out what it is, so that it is more user friendly and people don't feel guilty if they're not doing it all the time.

But if this generation cannot find out what sex really is then I would tell them that sex is like an onion. You peel it and peel it to find out what it is and all that you have left is a smell.'

Most of the class and Mrs Cassels were irritated by my conclusion.

'Sex is a serious matter, Jane. You can't compare it to an onion,' said Mrs Cassels.

Emily, one of the leading lights in the élite group, said, 'I don't see how she can write a whole report on something she hasn't done herself. I mean, at least Sophia travelled on a bus for Travel 2000, and I tested a lot of different food for Food 2000.' She was just saying that to be clever.

'Yes,' agreed Sophia, proving again what a lousy friend she was, 'how can she say it's not user friendly if she's never used it?'

Mrs Cassels, eyebrows ahoy, quickly said, 'No, no, no. It's perfectly proper to conduct a consumer survey from interviews alone. There was no requirement for Jane to test it personally.'

'I just think she should have been more respectful towards sex,' said one of the girls who'd frequently almost done it. 'It's a very important part of our lives.' Well she would say that wouldn't she?

They were all rather irritated by my report. I had the feeling that they all wanted to get their hands on it and put their own ideas in.

Therefore, after all that, my final conclusion was: It doesn't matter what you say about sex, it's going to annoy somebody.

☐ The Bumper Book of Erotic Failures	P. Kinnell	£4.99
☐ Modern Girls Book of Torture	Alison Everitt	£4.99
☐ The Condom Book for Girls	Alison Everitt	£3.99
☐ The Frog Factor	Serena Gray	£4.99
☐ Life's a Bitch ... And Then You Diet	Serena Gray	£3.99
☐ How Was It For You?	Maureen Lipman	£4.50

Warner Books now offers an exciting range of quality titles by both established and new authors which can be ordered from the following address:

Little, Brown & Company (UK),
P.O. Box 11,
Falmouth,
Cornwall TR10 9EN.

Alternatively you may fax your order to the above address.
Fax No. 01326 317444.

Payments can be made as follows: cheque, postal order (payable to Little, Brown and Company) or by credit cards, Visa/Access. Do not send cash or currency. UK customers and B.F.P.O. please allow £1.00 for postage and packing for the first book, plus 50p for the second book, plus 30p for each additional book up to a maximum charge of £3.00 (7 books plus). Overseas customers including Ireland, please allow £2.00 for the first book plus £1.00 for the second book, plus 50p for each additional book.

NAME (Block Letters) _____

ADDRESS _____

_____

_____

☐ I enclose my remittance for £ _____
☐ I wish to pay by Access/Visa Card

Number ☐☐☐☐☐☐☐☐☐☐☐☐☐☐☐☐

Card Expiry Date_____